M000198584

# A Dog of Few Words

## MARK SNYDER

A Dog of Few Words
Copyrighted © 2019 by Mark Snyder
ISBN 978-1-64538-092-4
First Edition

A Dog of Few Words
by Mark Snyder

For information, please contact:

Orange Hat Publishing
www.orangehatpublishing.com
Waukesha, WI

Cover design by Kaeley Dunteman
Edited by Lauren Blue

This novel is a work of fiction. The characters, locales, organizations, dialogue, incidents, and events portrayed in this novel are products of the author's imagination. Any references to real people or names of existing establishments are intended to give the fiction a sense of reality.

*For my brother, James Robert, and my grandchildren: Ross, Oliver, Nash, Maverick, and Sophia.*

# Introduction

This story is dedicated to the memory of pets present in our everyday lives and how they touch and communicate with us, whether they are a cat or dog, horse or pig, snake or turtle, or any other creature. They may not speak in human terms, but you can bet your britches they communicate in many other incredible ways. That's why we love them, and that's why we remember them long after they've gone. In fact, the inspiration for this novel came from a real-life companion mirrored in Abraham, the story's main pooch, that this family of eight loved so much as *a dog of few words.*

Hopefully, every reader will find something within these pages that touches their heart, makes them laugh, encourages them to listen to their surroundings, open their minds to learning something new once in a while, and live life to the fullest.

*Dogs are not our whole life,*
*but they make our lives whole. – Roger A Caras*

# Morning Companions

I was suddenly awakened by the swing of the bedroom door. It opened and closed without a sound as if someone or something had entered the room. The lack of light in the room did not help solve the mystery.

We always made sure that the bedroom door was closed each night. Not necessarily for privacy, contrary to what our children thought, but because the small hallway night-light at the top of the stairs would rudely cast its luminance across my pillow when the door was open. If the door was even cracked open one inch, the angle of the light would hit me right between the eyes. Darkness and quiet were always necessary at night to allow my senses to relax undisturbed. It was a personal thing, yes, and maybe I was oversensitive to light and noise at night, but that was just the fact. With kids sleeping just down the hall, a parent tends to sleep with one eye and one ear open at all times. The addition of a night-light shining on my noggin made for a cranky old man in the morning.

It was my nightly ritual to hang a bathrobe over the top of the bedroom door so as to prevent it from closing completely. This had two purposes. First, it allowed for a small amount of airflow to pass through the door opening. On windy winter nights, the bedroom was almost frigid in this old country farmhouse unless there was a cold air path to the register outside the door. Keeping the door from latching completely shut allowed warm air to flow from the heat duct and provided just enough warmth to sleep comfortably. Secondly, the robe on the door allowed Abraham to come and go as he pleased. Was it him, was there an intruder, was someone sick, did I imagine the door opening?

"Oooffff," I gasped when two large black paws took the air from my chest. "Good morning, Abe…is it that time already? Is it too much to ask for five more minutes? Did you plug the coffee in?"

As I glanced at the nightstand, I chuckled to myself for even looking at the clock. Of course, it was exactly 6:17am. If there was just one thing in life I could rely on, it was Abraham's punctuality in the early morning hours. I have never met a lab-pointer mix that could tell time, but he sure could. It started early in his young life when the alarm clock would sound at 6:30am each morning with its ear-piercing scream. Well, it must have been ear-piercing to him because he figured out how to prevent the alarm from ever sounding again. If he could turn the alarm clock off himself, I'm sure that he would have done just that. The next best thing was jumping on my chest at 6:17am each and every morning. Thus, he trained me to turn off the alarm before it even had a chance to sound. He was so reliable in his morning ritual that I stopped setting the alarm over a year ago.

As I lay there trying to drift back to sleep, I was hit by another blow to the chest followed by a cold, wet nose digging under the covers. "I'm up, I'm up!" I reluctantly declared. His left eye, which was now three inches from my nose, showed disbelief. As I tossed back the covers and swung a right leg over the side of the bed, his whole body exploded with excitement. Immediately, he returned to all fours, nudged open the door, and disappeared out into the hallway only to stick his head back in to assure me that he was not going downstairs without me. As I clumped down the stairs, I could hear him impatiently sounding the bells.

It was hard to tell what Abe wanted more in the morning, to be let outside or to be fed his one scoop of high-protein dog kibble. Years back, a decoration of Christmas sleigh bells had been hung on the inside of the back door. Abraham quickly learned that if he "chimed in" by nudging the bells with his nose, someone would let him outside. Later in life, he retrained the family to feed him at the sound of the bells. Having rung the bells two or three times, he would stand at the back door looking impatient. However, as soon as you reached for the door handle, he would pounce over to his empty dog bowl. If you opened the door and called to him, he would look at you like you were crazy. He didn't want to go out, he wanted his kibble. It's funny how after five years we are still trained to come to his aid at the ringing of the bells, which he has been doing for the last two minutes straight now.

Since the wife and kids are not morning people, it was usually up to the two of us, man and dog, to get things started. I plug in the coffee percolator, and Abe polishes off that scoop of dog food. He makes the rounds outside, and I hit the bathroom. I turn the lights on and open the curtains, and he pounces on the kids, pulling at their blankets. If I went outside, he went outside. If I watch TV, he watches TV. If I was enjoying a snack, he was at my feet trying to enjoy it also. And so it went every morning, rain and shine, cold and warm, summer and winter. The only thing better than a busy weekday morning for man and his best friend was the weekend when things slowed down a bit. I would enjoy a long cup of coffee and a song on my baritone ukulele. Abe would lie across my lap in front of the woodstove, tolerating the wrong notes and off-key singing while he listened for the pitter-patter of little feet getting out of bed above us. Mornings meant we were inseparable. We were morning companions!

*The older you get, the more
you realize you don't know. – Opa*

# The Whistle-Pig

Have you ever woken up not in a hurry to do anything in particular, but having the itch to do something? That was exactly what my inner voice was telling me this morning as I looked out the kitchen window that faced the back forty. There was still snow on the ground in late February, and the sun was creating a purple, orange, and yellow sunrise. Abe seemed antsy to get outside for the second time, and my third cup of coffee was empty. As soon as I grabbed my snow boots, Abe's ears perked right up. He knew that meant something different about today...could it be...sure enough...it was a Saturday!

Abraham wasn't much for words, but his body was telling me that he very much agreed with my decision. His squirming got worse when I had trouble finding a pair of work gloves that matched. For some unknown reason, it seemed like every pair of gloves was missing the right hand. Sort of like when that sock goes missing after laundry day. My choice of winter gloves was inexpensive yellow work gloves that were purchased in packs of ten pairs from the local farm store. I could not believe that every pair that I located in the cedar wooden crate where we stored them was missing the right hand. Abe decided I was taking too long and wanted to help. Soon his black nose was buried in the glove crate, which caused him to sneeze twice. "There's one!" I exclaimed. He immediately latched onto it with his front teeth as if to say he had found it himself. I stuffed a couple peanut butter sandwiches in my coat pocket, and out we went.

Maple syrup time was fast approaching here in southern Wisconsin. This is the time of year when the temperature starts below freezing at night but the morning sun quickly warms the day above the freezing temperature of 32 degrees Fahrenheit. This thermal fluctuation seems to wake everything up in nature. The sap begins to flow in the maples, the birds begin to migrate north, the grass begins peeking through the snow, and man and his dog, suffering from a three-month cabin fever, get restless to explore the woods and hills. This morning, I wanted to check on the sugar maples at the back of our property. I thought about getting the David Brown tractor out of the shed, but I was expecting a fast warm-up today, which meant slush and ruts. Melting snow can get you stuck without warning, especially when the tire tread has seen its better days. On this day, walking was definitely going to be the mode of travel. Abraham was ecstatic and quickly began dragging around a large branch that had fallen near the back of the barn.

I'm not sure which one of us spotted her first, but both of us froze in our tracks. Directly in front of us, not fifteen feet away, was a very large woodchuck climbing over a half-debarked fallen box elder log. She was gorgeous. How gorgeous, you ask? Well, as gorgeous as a woodchuck can be. She stiffly moved about, having just emerged from her winter den. She stretched, yawned, and scratched but with gentleness and elegance. Abe, with his ears back, looked like he was ready to give chase. I slowly kneeled down and placed my left arm over his front shoulders to let him know that I disagreed with his impulse to rip her to shreds. His whole body was shaking with excitement, and he was whining in rhythm with every quiver. My movement was enough for this reddish-gray whistle-pig to lock her beautiful brown eyes on us. Now we were stuck in a ten-foot, don't blink, three-way stare down.

To my surprise, she did not let out the infamous high-pitch alarm that gave groundhogs their nickname. Instead, she remained perfectly still. I was curious to see how patient she was, convinced that man and domesticated dog could outstare a wild animal. But wouldn't you know it, I soon felt a leg cramp coming on and knew I had to move. I had been kneeling on the ground for the last ten minutes, and my left leg, at first cold and wet because of the snow, was now completely numb. Frustrated that I was about to lose the challenge, I braced my left arm on Abraham's back and was just about to stand up when I heard a soft, sweet, gentle voice say, "So now what?"

Now, I know my blood circulation was cut off to my left leg, but to my noggin? I looked around and confirmed that no one else was around. No kids, no wife, nobody except the three of us. I looked back at the wild animal in front of me. She was still as frozen as before until her head rose up ever so slowly so that her eyes looked directly into mine, and she said, "Call off the dog, mister...I don't want to hurt him."

Well, you can imagine my astonishment having just heard a woodchuck speak. I wondered if I was still asleep. Maybe Abe did not wake me up at 6:17am like he always did. Could I be dreaming? Did he let me sleep in for once? But then I heard a different voice come from beneath me. This one was deeper in pitch, almost kid-like, with a weird accent. I thought I heard it mumble, "You wish!" Did my dog just answer that woodchuck? I looked down at him, and he was licking his chops, no longer shaking.

My right leg buckled and my body collapsed, not because of the cold or lack of circulation, but because I was shaking like the dog had been a few minutes ago. At this point, the woodchuck disappeared over the log and Abe turned his attention to me, licking my face. Within a few minutes, I regained my composure. I was able to stand, and Abraham quickly brought me another stick, even bigger than the last one.

I managed to stumble over to the half-rotten box elder log, and I sat down to ponder things for a minute. Abe, now sitting in front of me with that goofy stick in his mouth, began wagging his tail like nothing in the world was any different than any other day. I took my yellow work gloves off and tucked them in a coat pocket. As I did, I felt the edge of a sandwich in my pocket. I pulled it out, unwrapped the white butcher paper, and took a few bites. I was so deep in thought that I didn't even comprehend if the sandwich had any flavor. For all I knew, I was eating one of my work gloves.

*NEVER stop playing, WAG more BARK less,*
*Be LOYAL and FAITHFUL, Be Quick to Forgive*
*and Love UNCONDITIONALLY*
*– Author Unknown ("Lessons I Learned from my Dog")*

# Abe and Ada

Abraham was a good dog most of the time, unusually good. Better than most dogs I have met or owned. However, once in a while, but not very often, I would find Abe in his kennel when I got home from work, sent there by my lovely bride Dona. He never went to his kennel unless someone yelled at him for something silly, like sleeping on a blanket that wasn't his or eating the cat food that belonged to our three cats, Sam, Gimli, and Norm, things that seemed silly to Abe but somehow were not silly to the wife. He would hide behind me with head hung low while Dona explained what "my dog" had done during the day to deserve such a punishment as being kenneled.

As I said, he was a great dog, and he did tricks too. The kids had taught him to do several simple tricks like the standard lay down, sit, high five, shake, and "speak." One trick that Dona taught him was to "say please" by softly smacking his lips without barking when he wanted a treat or a piece of food you were eating.

That got me to thinking...I had food in my hand. Abraham was attentively watching me eat said food while he sat in front of me with a desperate look of want in his eyes and a line of drool coming from his mouth. Time for a man-to-dog, heart-to-heart, food-to-stomach talk! So, I pulled the second sandwich out of my coat pocket, unwrapped it, and said, "I'll give you this whole peanut butter sandwich if you talk. Not *speak*, not *say please*, but TALK like I just heard you talk."

Nothing...nothing but his normal double smack of the mouth saying "please" as Dona had taught him. I assured him that this was a confidential conversation and that I would never tell anyone. That it was just between him and me. All I wanted was to hear him say one human word in exchange for the entire second sandwich. He would gain by winning the prize, and I would gain by knowing that I'm not insane after all. Still nothing...nothing but lip smacking and drool.

"I'll take it," said that same soft, gentle voice I had heard before. I turned sharply to my left, and there was that woodchuck with her front feet up on the same log I was sitting on. Her head was facing me as her eye contact moved from the sandwich to my eyes. Again, she said, "I'll take it, please."

Stunned as I was, I laid the entire second sandwich in front of her. She slowly reached out with her mouth and took a bite. Abraham let out a shrill bark, and my attention immediately turned back to him.

Now certain that both had spoken, I pointedly asked Abraham why he had never spoken to me in the past. "Don't know," he grumbled as he watched the woodchuck quickly finish off the entire sandwich.

"Don't know?" I stammered back. "Don't know? Is that all you have to say to a loyal friend who has covered your tracks more than once, who has bailed you out of trouble with the wife, who has let you jump on the bed to sleep on a warm blanket after the Mrs. has fallen asleep? Who always saves the last bite for you? Who puts up with the dog slobber on the car windows and the muddy paw prints on the seat? Need I say more?" With that, Abe went back to tossing a stick up in the air and trying to catch it.

Well, that was the bulk of my Saturday morning. I never dreamed I would have a conversation with my own dog and a two-year-old woodchuck named Ada that lived under a woodpile behind my barn. I spent most of the day with these two characters. I found out that Abe is a dog of few words. In fact, I don't think I heard him say another word all day. Ada, on the other hand, appears at first to be gentle and shy but is direct and outgoing. Like a lot of females, she says what's on her mind. Abe is all about fun, and Ada is all about food. Abe usually has a rock or stick in his mouth, and Ada likes to eat dandelions, clover heads, and almost anything else that is growing behind the old barn.

*If you don't have a dog, at least one, there is not necessarily anything wrong with you. But there may be something wrong with your life. – Vincent Van Gogh*

# The Love Shack

To catch you up to speed, it was now nine days later. February 28th to be precise! The midday temperatures were warming up nicely. Today's forecast was for the low 40's and lots of sun. That, to me, meant it was time to tap the maple trees.

Some say February is too early to tap the maples in Wisconsin, that there is a chance that the 3/8-inch hole drilled into a tree trunk will close up by the end of sap season if tapped too early, but I was looking forward to an early spring. The first sap out of a sugar maple makes the best syrup, has the best color, and has the best flavor. Early sap sometimes produces golden syrup with a blonde-brown color.

The envied golden syrup can only be obtained if the sugar content of the sap is extremely high. Sugar maple trees in Wisconsin normally have a sap that is forty-to-one, forty gallons of sap producing one gallon of syrup. However, golden syrup is made from a sap that has about a thirty-to-one ratio, which means less boiling of the sap. Understandably, less boiling of the sap produces lighter-colored syrup and has less caramelization. The resulting heavenly flavor is something few people have experienced. A backyard syrup maker like me will hoard golden syrup for his own private stock, thinking that most people would never appreciate such a delicacy. They say in marriage, "happy wife...happy life." In maple syrup production, or sugaring as it is called, we say "early tap...golden sap."

Who better to ask about the chances of an early spring than a woodchuck, right? So, Abe and I headed out behind the old dairy barn this morning to find Ada. Just about to leave the house, as we neared the back door, we were sternly reminded by the Mrs. that she wanted neither muddy man nor muddy dog prints across her kitchen floor today. Abe impatiently rang the Christmas bells on the doorknob as I acknowledged her with a naughty, deceitful grin as if to say, "There are guarantees from neither man nor his dog, but we love you just the same."

As I grabbed my favorite green hooded jacket with front zipper and my Wisconsin-made red and black Stormy Kromer hat, I recalled that I had not seen Ada in the last two days. Every day since we met, I would see her as she rounded the southeast corner of the barn just after sunrise. From the bay window in the kitchen, I'd say, "There's Ada," interrupting Abe's morning kibble inhalation while I sipped on a steaming hot, black cup of joe. Abe would trot over to the window, jump up with front paws on the sill, and peek around the curtain. Soon his black tail would be twitching, and his ears would perk up. I couldn't hear a thing, but he would listen intently as if she were talking to him in some frequency inaudible to old human ears. Since Ada was endowed with the "gift of gab," she was probably just talking to herself each morning, and I assumed all was well if Abe returned to his bowl of kibble a few seconds later.

Before checking in with Ada this morning, we took a short detour and grabbed some tools from the sugar shack. The sugar shack was straight west of the back door and a little north of the barn. It was the old fifteen-by-ten-foot granary for the farm. It had a thick corrugated metal roof just like the barn, and today's sunshine reflected off its silver color with a blinding glare. Its barnboards were bare of any paint, and its battens were broken, if not mostly missing. This made for a very airy building, perfect for sugaring. The floorboards had rotted away years ago, leaving behind a dirt floor full of old odds and ends buried beneath its surface.

By strategically placing cinder blocks in a rectangular six-by-four-foot pattern four cinder blocks high, we made an inexpensive firebox for sugaring right in the middle of the dirt floor. The front had a tin sheet across a two-foot opening to allow for adding wood, and the back had a metal top and a stovepipe attached. We used two stainless steel eight-inch-deep sugar pans that were two-foot-wide and three-foot long. They were placed on top of the firepit and filled with maple sap. Once a roaring hot fire was built, so hot that the stovepipe was crimson red, the sap would come to a rolling boil. Water vapor filled the entire building and escaped through the broken battens and from under the metal roof. It was a glorious sight! Our usual syrup production yielded from seven to nine gallons of syrup, equating to the boiling of about 350 gallons of maple sap, so it was important that we check our cooking equipment and wood stock today.

Upon opening the sugar shack door this morning, I immediately realized that something was amok. Right there in the middle of the dirt floor was a great big hole and a large pile of recently excavated dirt. The angle of the hole went under the front left corner of the cinder block firebox. Abe saw it before I did and cautiously stepped forward to investigate. When he reached the pile of dirt, he suddenly stopped. I saw the long black hairs on his back stand straight up. That was NOT a good sign! While it was obvious that some animal had dug a very large hole, it also became clear that Abraham did not know who or what it was. He froze in his "I'm scared" stance and began to do his nervous quivering, just like the first time he met Ada. Soon he began to snort and sneeze as he intently tried to use his Sherlock nose to decipher this mystery.

"What is it, Abe?" I asked him.

My dog of few words softly and repeatedly muttered, "Don't know...don't know...don't know...don't know."

I walked up beside him, knelt down, and put my hand around his left side. He was shaking like a leaf! We both stared down that hole like we were waiting for something to pop out at us when suddenly I felt something brush up against my leg from behind me. I jumped to my feet and let out some kind of inhuman noise along with a few choice words. Abe jumped twice as high as I did and let out a confused bark about three octaves higher than normal. Just then, I heard the sound of Ada's sweet, calm voice come from under me. She was humming or singing or cooing or something. She brushed in between Abe and me and crawled right down the hole, out of sight. Abe let out another loud bark, but this time his voice was back to normal. After he regained his full composure, he began to sniff at the dirt pile once again. His head tilted a little sideways, and he gave me a confused look. He didn't ask anything with his mouth, but his whole body was saying, "What in tarnation was that?" After a few more confusing moments, I softly but firmly exclaimed, "Ada, will you please tell us what is going on?"

Almost immediately, I heard some rustling from inside the firebox. Within seconds, a whiskery, dirt-covered nose emerged from the hole. It was Ada. She climbed to the top of the dirt pile, collapsed in a heap, and said, "I'm in love!"

I reached over and grabbed a five-gallon bucket to sit on. Abe went nose-to-nose with Ada on the dirt pile and said very sarcastically, "Do tell."

After a half hour of sappy conversation, we concluded that Ada had found a boyfriend. This so-called boyfriend was the one responsible for the big hole under our cinder block firepit. It appeared that he had visited the farm a few days ago, found a willing woodchuck to wine and dine, dug her a mating den, and currently was nowhere to be found. Yes, it was going to be an early spring, for love was in the air, or at least in the love shack…I mean sugar shack.

Abe was not amused with Ada's antics and attempted to backfill the hole with her still in it. Dirt was flying everywhere. I reminded him that the Mrs. was going to make him, and probably me also, sleep in the barn if he got all dirty. Besides the gaping hole in the floor, the left front corner of the firepit had some rodent damage. After further investigation, we located another hole under the north wall of the granary that the lovers had been using to gain access into the building. I told both Abe and Ada to vacate the "love shack" and that I would fill in the hole myself with some gravel as soon as…

well, as soon as the gravel pile thawed out. Relieved that Ada was ok and nothing expensive had been damaged, I turned my attention to the sugaring equipment.

*Old Groundhog stretched in his leafy bed,*
*He turned over slowly and then he said,*
*"I wonder if spring is on the way,*
*I'll go and check the weather today..."*
*– Author Unknown ("Groundhog Day")*

# The Prophet

"Abe, you wanna go outside?"

Come to think of it, I bet I'd said that three thousand times. "Abe, you wanna go outside?" was declared each and every day, if not ten times a day. This day started the same way. The response was usually the same, and in this order: ears come up, jump off the dog bed, and run to the back door. I could ask from the kitchen, the living room, or the bedroom. I could shout it, whisper it, or even think it, and Abe would respond. He could be snoring louder than the dishwasher and still hear me ask, "Abe, you wanna go outside?"

However, today was different. I asked the question from the kitchen over my second cup of coffee, but there was no response. I walked to the living room, but Abe wasn't on his dog bed by the woodstove. I asked a second time, but my summons waged no reply. Curiously, I investigated. I found him with front paws up on the dining room windowsill looking out at the front yard. "What's up?" I asked. "Is Penelope out this morning?"

I joined Abe at the window with my cup of coffee in hand. Penelope was the red fox squirrel that had a home in the ash leaf maple by the mailbox. For some reason, she preferred to make her home in a branch that hung out over the road in front of our farmhouse. She had two entrances, one under the branch, which was the front door, and one at the end of the dead branch, which was only used when unwanted company visited. On most sunny mornings, she would emerge right after sunrise. She would yawn and stretch and slowly meander from limb to limb and lap up water that collected in the divots of the soft maple. After chewing on a few maple buds, she would swirl around and around the tree trunk, making her way to the grass below. Watching her leap across the lawn was another routine Abe and I shared most mornings, but that is another story for another time. No, today the action that held Abe's attention was at the bird feeder.

Any farmer will tell you that animals act differently when the weather is about to change. I swear that watching animals, particularly birds, is a better way to predict and prepare for an incoming weather front than any forecast on the TV or radio. Bird activity is certainly not a difficult thing to observe, but it can be a challenge to interpret. What the commotion really means might have you scratching your head at times. I was reaching up to pat Abe's hairy, black head when he said one simple word, "See!"

It only took me seconds to reach the same page that Abe was on. As I moved my eyes to follow where Abe was looking, I almost spilled my coffee. What we saw was astonishing! It was ALL happening at the bird feeders! "Good Lord, Abe, what is going on?"

"Don't know," he said. "Don't know."

Before us, not five feet from the window, was a plethora of activity. The twins were there, Rubin was there, Spike was there, and Harry and Sally were there. Svetlana and Bartholomew were there. Even Jerry was there! This was a spectacular sight. Not that so many birds were at the feeders, but that they were all there at the same time, along with everyone else on the farm! You see, the bird feeder was one thing on the farm that required a hierarchy of order. To see everyone at the feeders at once was very unusual. In fact, I don't think we had ever seen such a display before. And Jerry never showed up until after dark. But we need to back up a bit here and do some splainin'.

Each morning at sunrise, the first bird to the feeders was Spike, a beautiful crimson-red cardinal. Spike was a very young and handsome dude with a crown gelled into a perfect spike at the top of his head, as if he had just come from the salon. If he was courting, then he would stand guard while his girlfriend was permitted to pick at the feeder undisturbed. If any other creature even dared to approach, Spike was set in motion. The twins, two black-capped chickadees, would usually show up next, followed by Rubin the red-bellied woodpecker and sometimes joined by Harry and Sally.

The woodpeckers were always a favorite at the feeders, but Harry and Sally especially. They were a mating pair of hairy woodpeckers and made a cute couple. Instead of landing on the feeders, they would land under the feeders and peek their heads up to grab a morsel. Then they would quickly fly to the mulberry tree to enjoy their take, returning seconds later. They were very selective about what they took from the feeders but were the most polite of any birds at the feeders. Waiting their turn was no problem at all. Golden finches and red finches got along gloriously too, not only with each other but with everyone else also. Since they had their own feeder filled with thistle seed, they seldom competed in the hierarchy at the feeders. Even the field sparrows and nuthatches shared the feeders with genuine etiquette. Those rabid house sparrows were usually the ones causing most of the problem!

When house sparrows arrived at the feeders, everyone else disappeared. They were rude and mean. The males were the absolute worst. They gorged themselves even before they let the ladies have a turn. They threw seed out of the feeders and made a mess of everything. No bird dared to alight at the feeders until the house sparrows were done eating!

Soon after the morning rush hour at the feeders was over, Svetlana and her son Bartholomew would show up. Svety and Barth were the clean-up crew underneath the feeders. They were thirteen-lined striped gophers that lived in the old pine log in the front yard. Two years ago, a lightning storm took down this thirty-foot ponderosa. Over the years, most of the wood had been used for campfire wood. All that remained now was a portion of the rotting stump, which made an excellent home for our resident gophers. They had a sweet tooth for sunflower seeds, but were happy to try just about anything that fell from the master's table. They spent an hour or two each day packing seeds back to the ponderosa homestead. Every now and then, I catch Bartholomew lazily planting his seeds instead of trekking back to the stump. Thanks to him, we had some nice millet and sunflower plants during the summer to spruce up the feeder site. But I digress…

The last creature to peruse the bird feeders most days, well after the cat dish on the back step, was Jerry the possum. She was whitish/gray and very large, and she seemed to eat about everything. She lived somewhere on the farm, but we had never discovered where. She was very secretive and very slow. On several occasions, I had been able to sneak right up to her. She usually hissed and showed her teeth and then slowly waddled off to the nearest tree. She wasn't the prettiest face on the farm, but she was a regular visitor and as welcome as any other.

To my surprise, as I started to say, there was a most spectacular sight at the feeders this morning that had attracted Abe's, and now my, attention. Instead of the usual bickering and fighting, the waiting and retreating, the "me first" attitude of some and the "I'm too shy" of others, they were all at the feeders at the same time. I couldn't believe my eyes. Spike was there, along with three other cardinals, the house and field sparrows were there, Harry and Sally were flying back and forth from the mulberry along with Rubin, the twins' entire family seemed to be present, along with finches, a nuthatch we named Bobber, two downy woodpeckers, one crow, a crowd of starlings, and a flock of dark-eyed juncos. Svety and Barth were busy right beside Jerry, Penny, and two gray squirrels we had never seen before. An unbelievable sight!

Just when I thought I had seen everything, I saw Ada out of the corner of my eye, lingering near the arborvitae. "She came to the front yard, Abe!" I declared. "I don't think I have ever seen Ada in the front yard! The world must be coming to an end! Let's go talk to her." Abe immediately jumped down from the windowsill and headed to the back door.

I warned Abe to leave the bird feeder activity alone. I didn't want a dog or squirrel turned into asphalt on the road. To my advantage, Abe had already found the cat food dish and was busy cleaning up any breakfast morsels that may have been passed up by our tabby, Norman. Slowly, I crept around the south side of the house to get Ada's attention without flustering the feeder frenzy. I was concerned about spooking Ada, but of course, she knew I was there long before I reached the arborvitae.

"What's up, big guy!" she squeaked. "Got any sandwiches on you?"

"No, Ada, I don't...sorry...maybe later at lunchtime I can smuggle one out of the house for you," I whispered. "What's all the hubbub at the bird feeder this morning? I've never seen one, but that's got all the ear marks of a run!"

"Oh, it's something all right, coming from the east this time," Ada fired back. "Mother Nature has an early squall coming our way! I heard that crow blabbing, 'Nevermore... Nevermore!' and something about his last meal before Armageddon. Come to think of it, I have an awful stomachache this morning. You sure you don't have a sandwich on you?"

"So are we talking inches or feet of snow," I inquired curiously, "cause I already took the snow blade off the tractor."

"Not sure, but I might just sleep in a day or two. Doubt if we'll see the grass for a while. You better get me a couple sandwiches please!" she flirted as she batted her beautiful brown eyes at me.

Abe and I kept the feeders full that morning and found a stale loaf of bread for Ada. Sure enough, not a half hour later, it started snowing big, fluffy, white flakes. By noon, the schools were closed, and by 2pm, the highways were closed.

It caught everyone off guard! The radio forecast wasn't even close. Makes you wonder why everyone doesn't have a bird feeder in their front yard. It wouldn't hurt to make friends with a chubby prophetic woodchuck either.

*Oh, how delightful one sandwich can be. Delicious,*
*delightful, having been stuffed with cheese! – Opa*

# Grilled Cheese

Indeed, today was the day! Time to tap the maple trees! The sun was quickly warming the frozen tundra. The blackbirds, starlings, and cowbirds were joyfully declaring their presence in the front yard. The remaining snow was quickly turning to slush, and the icicles hanging from the barn roof where dripping quite rapidly. At first, I didn't notice the icicles, but Abe was just about skewered by one as it crashed to the ground when I opened the hayloft door. He made a sudden leap sideways and let out a loud "Yipe!" as he crashed into my right leg. The cement stoop of the barn I was standing on was slick with a water-covered ice sheet, and both dog and man ended up "ass over tea kettle." I'm not sure which one of us was the ass and which one was the tea kettle, but the lovestruck woodchuck was beside herself with laughter as we attempted to right our bruised bodies. I lashed out at her with a quote from the movie *Star Wars*, saying, "Laugh it up, fuzzball" and proceeded to wipe out on the ice a second time, making sure to take both dog and fuzzball down with me.

The third attempt, while not very graceful, was more successful. I quickly hobbled to the garage, grabbed a bag of rock salt, and coated the cement. After putting the bag away inside the barn, I noticed that Abraham was not with me. I walked to the hayloft door and saw him staring at the salt-covered cement. In my frustration, I had forgotten how he hates to walk on salt in the winter. It dries the pads on his feet so that the salt gets into the cracks of his toes. He never complains, but it must hurt something fierce. Sometimes I would see him hold up a paw and lick it to get the salt out. I bet that tasted terrible. He turned his stare at the salt to a stare directly at me. "Sorry, I forgot," I declared and quickly found a broom to clear a path for his delicate, black, hairy paws. With legs spread apart, claws fully extended, head lowered, he gingerly shuffled across the icy stoop.

Inside the barn loft, Abe helped me remove the white canvas tarp that covered the sugaring equipment by growling and tugging. Mumbling to myself, I reviewed a mental checklist to affirm that all necessary hardware was present and accounted for: buckets, spiles, sap tank, my grandpa's antique hand drill with 3/8-inch bit, five-gallon pails with lids, and a few 35-gallon plastic garbage containers. "Looks like it's all here," I said and began carrying everything to the hayloft door.

After the fourth or fifth trip, I noticed that Abe was gone. I didn't think much about it, expecting that he was out bugging Ada or digging salt from between his toes. However, after I had moved all the sugaring equipment to the sugar shack, it surprised me that he had not returned. While he often goes exploring, his separation anxiety gets the best of him and he quickly returns to check on me; most of the time he is away from my side less than five minutes before he checks in. It dawned on me that he had been gone for better than a half hour.

Just as I closed the hayloft door, Dona yelled from the back door that she would have tomato soup and hot grilled cheese sandwiches ready in about five minutes. I hollered back to see if Abe was in the house.

She shrugged her shoulders and shouted that she hadn't seen him. "Well, not since I saw you and him do the glacier slip 'n slide at the barn door a half hour ago," she chuckled.

"Thanks," I stammered, "we'll be in for lunch in a few minutes."

If anyone knew anything about the farm, it would be Ada, so I headed to the woodpile behind the barn. Sure enough, she was exactly where I expected to find her...in the garden. I walked right up to her before she noticed me, which startled her. She had her nose buried in the dirt as she meticulously attempted to dig up a frozen carrot.

"Starting a little early on my vegetables, aren't you?" I asked.

With her mouth full, she fired back, "What's yours is mine."

"Have you seen Abe in the last half hour?"

"Nope," she replied and went right back to digging.

Sarcastically, as I began to walk away, I announced, "Thanks for your help."

All of a sudden, she balanced on her hind legs and squeaked out, "Wait, I hear barking from the road."

I had to listen attentively, since Ada's hearing is much keener than mine, but I could faintly hear something that sounded like dog, but it wasn't barking, was it? I quickly headed back around the barn, down the gravel driveway, past the old farmhouse, and out toward the road.

Our property was located on a blacktopped country road. Well, at one time it was blacktopped. Since our township had financial challenges and had not touched this road in many, many years, it was now so full of potholes and cracks that it was slowly turning into granulized tar balls, not what I would call blacktop. You would think that the dangerous status of the road would slow traffic down, but au contraire! It just keeps the auto mechanics in business replacing all the tires and shocks that this road destroys. I know this all too well as a father of a driving-age teenager. Just last year, the neighbor's telephone pole was compromised when a driver lost control of her compact vehicle on a busted-up piece of road. It was a work of art how she wrapped it around the pole. I looked up and down the road, but there was no dog anywhere to be seen.

As I approached the mailbox, I could now hear muffled but excited barking. It sounded like it was coming from the ground under my feet. "How is that even possible?" I uttered to myself. I knelt to the ground, and sure enough, Abe was under my feet, under the road, barking his fool head off. I looked to the side of the ditch by the mailbox and noticed that the gravel had been disturbed. After further investigation, I found that the entrance to an old metal culvert had been dug out. The road was so deteriorated that I didn't even know there was a culvert. It was buried from years of neglect and rusted near oblivion. I flopped down on my stomach and began to look into the end of the recently excavated culvert. Abe was definitely in there, and he was definitely upset about something.

"Abe, what's going on?" I yelled. "You stuck?"

The barking stopped, and I could hear Abe working his way toward me. Slowly, he backed out of the small six-inch diameter hole as I dug around him and pulled him out by his tail. Tongue hanging out of his mouth, covered in dirt and cobwebs over his entire body, he repeatedly panted, "Found him…found him…found him." And then he proceeded to bark into the hole just like before.

"Found who? I thought you were stuck in there? Why didn't you come and get me? What…what's going on? By the way, the Mrs. has grilled cheese sandwiches ready."

At that, it was like his brain switched circuits. He looked straight at my face, sucked in his tongue, licked his chops, and ran for the house. It seemed that lunch was more important than what he had found in the culvert, which, by the way, was Ada's newfound love…Señor Woodchuck.

Needless to say, this was the day when the husband was privileged to eat his lunch on the back porch instead of at the kitchen table. According to the wife, "A dog full of mud and cobwebs is not allowed in the house, and the man who allowed this to happen can eat with his dog." I have to confess that that was the best lunch we'd had in a long time. You just can't beat a couple of hot grilled cheese sandwiches on the back step with man's best friend.

We never heard from "Señor Woodchuck" again!

*The best time to plant a maple tree is twenty years ago.*
*The second-best time is now! – Opa*

# Tapping the Maples

After lunch, I loaded up all the maple tree tapping equipment in the loader of the David Brown 990 tractor and headed out to the back forty. Actually, I don't know why I call it the back forty because we don't own anywhere near forty acres of land. I guess it was just a saying I'd learned in my youth after spending time on the farm.

Grandpa was to blame, or rather Grandpa was the one to thank. I learned a lot of things about nature and animals and life from my grandpa. He taught me important things like how not to stand directly behind a cow when it coughs, that an east rain is going to be a long and wet rain, and how to make Grandma laugh even when she is mad.

Pulling my leg was his favorite pastime. One day when I was about twelve, I spent the good part of two hours trying to convince my grandpa that Wisconsin whitetail buck deer lose their antlers each winter and grow a new rack of antlers in the spring. He led on like it was the craziest thing he had ever heard. On another day, when he took me fishing, I had forgotten to bring the angleworms that we had dug from Grandma's garden. Completely crushed that I had ruined our fishing day, he quickly showed me how to find worms under logs. That day we brought home our limit of fish! Thinking of Grandma cooking us those bluegills reminds me of their modest house in the Baraboo Hills. It smelled of wood smoke even in the summer. The same smell I hoped to create under a pan of maple sap real soon.

So out to the back forty, or rather the back ten, to tap the sugar maples. Tapping is pretty easy, but it does take some observations. It helps if you "pay attention" to what nature is showing you out in the woods. First of all, it is pretty important that you be able to identify the difference between a sugar maple, an oak, an ash, or any other similarly barked tree. It is surprising how difficult it is, even for an expert like Abe, to identify a tree without any leaves on the branches. You would be very hard-pressed to get sap out of a white oak. I know this because I have a brother-in-law in Minnesota who accidentally tried it once. Secondly, it pays to study the entire maple tree before drilling a hole for a tap or spile.

Only from experience, aka trial and error, did Abe and I learn which of our trees were good sap producers and which ones were not. It also helps to look up once in a while. A tree that has lost its top or is full of rot will most likely produce little sap. Besides that, there are probably a few squirrels or raccoons that live in said tree. Squirrels, while one of God's great creations, were not our friends during sugaring. They loved to pee on our bucket lids and chew holes in the sugaring equipment as they attempted to get at the sweet, sugary, concentrated maple sap.

Within ten minutes, we arrived in the "sugar bush." I

parked the tractor on the south end of the tree line as usual, and Abe went off exploring. As I walked through the trees, clearing debris from around the trunks, I carried with me the three things necessary to tap a tree. With me today, I had a pocket full of spiles, my grandpa's trusty hand drill, and a claw hammer on my belt. Starting on the north end of the woods, I worked my way back to the tractor.

It usually goes like this. First, I find last year's tap holes and make sure they are healed shut; if not, I skip that tree for one year. Second, I try to go above or below last year's mark and four or five inches left or right, angle the bit of the drill slightly upward, and drill to a designated depth marked on the drill bit. On a warm, sunny day when the temperature is above 40 degrees Fahrenheit, sap should immediately run from the drilled hole and self-clean it of wood chips. Grabbing a spile from my pocket, I tap it gently into the 3/8-inch hole until snug.

I must have been in good spirits today because it only took me one hour to get forty-five taps ready for buckets. Abe came over a few times to check my progress. Satisfied that I was doing it right, he just headed off with nose to the ground, stopping once in a while to circle a tree trunk. I think he was attempting to locate that nasty fox squirrel that irritates us year after year. Unfortunately, this elusive squirrel changes his residence each year. Sometimes he lives in "old faithful" on the south end, the largest maple that out-produces the other trees. Some years, he moves to the north end of the woods. Wherever he is, he always pees on our bucket lids and sometimes pries off lids to drink the sap. I threaten him every year that I'm gonna bring a gun, but I never do.

Since I had worked my way back to the tractor, I grabbed an armful of buckets and lids. This was the fun part because it goes quickly and creates a chorus of music in the woods as the sap hits the bottom of an empty metal pail. I energetically hung the sap buckets on the spiles and covered each one with a lid. Stopping at the far end of the woods, I could hear the "plink" of sap dripping into the forty-five buckets. It was a glorious sound to hear in the woods, music to my ears. It sounded like a *golden* year to me!

Just as I was positioning the last lid, I heard the second sound of spring, not coming from the "plink" of sap but from the sky. A flock of sandhill cranes were coming in from the south. It sounded like all of them were singing at the same time, probably as happy as I was that spring had arrived in the frozen tundra of Wisconsin.

The third and final sound of spring that I long for after a long winter usually comes near the end of sugaring. This sound comes after a warm spring rain when most of the snow has melted. It's the choir of the frogs in the slough behind our woods. That's when Abe and I are convinced that spring has sprung in Wisconsin!

Satisfied that our work was done, I gave a verbal warning to Mr. Fox Squirrel as I yelled through the trees and turned the 990 back toward home. Abe was already leading the way, ears flopping, covered in mud, and a stick in his mouth.

*You had me at "candied bacon"*
*(bacon cooked in maple syrup) – Opa*

# Four Buffalo Syrup

It was raining today, the Ides of March. As I leaned on the door of the sugar shack, I reflected that it could be worse. It could be snowing in mid-March. Mud, it was everywhere. The snow was all but gone, the frost in the ground was thawed, and the frogs in the slough were singing their songs of love. Abe and I spent the last three weeks chopping wood, collecting sap, boiling, boiling, and more boiling. We already bottled twenty-one quart jars of *special reserve* golden syrup and hoped to finish off the rest of the maple syrup today. Every winter, I couldn't wait to get out in the woods to make syrup, but by the end of sugaring, I would be tired and my muscles would be sore. I was looking forward to the end of a good sugar season. The first few years we made syrup, everyone in the household wanted to help. Now it was just the Mrs., the dog, and the tired old man. Well, just the tired old man today. Even Abe was inside the house, curled up on his bed, nose tucked under his tail, fast asleep. Not a bad idea on a rainy, damp, spring day like today.

The firebox under the syrup pan was now just a bed of red-hot coals. Every five minutes or so, I threw in a few small, finger-sized, dry box elder sticks on the hot coals to excite the boil. It was getting close; the bubbles in the sugar pan were much smaller than when the sap first came to a boil two days ago. That meant that there was more concentration of sugar and less water in the pan. The boiling point of syrup is about seven degrees Fahrenheit higher than the boiling point of water. When the process got this close, I didn't dare take my eyes off the pan.

There was less than an inch of liquid in the eight-inch-deep sugar pan. I was watching for a flare-up. This happened when a hot spot of coals under the pan caused the syrup to over-boil. If this happened, there were only seconds to spare before the syrup boiled into candy. The easiest way to calm the syrup was to immediately dribble some fresh sap into the pan. I'd heard stories that people burned their houses down when they had a boil-over on the kitchen stove.

The smell of sweet syrup in the sugar shack almost makes your mouth drool with anticipation. I have to admit that I sampled the taste quite often. This batch had a little more caramelization and a much darker color than the first batch we finished last Thursday. Nevertheless, it still tasted mighty good!

There were several ways to test the syrup for readiness. My grandpa, the great storyteller, taught me the *buffalo* method of sugaring. This was said to be the first ever method of testing syrup for sugar content used by the Native Americans of Wisconsin. While the origin of the story may be authentic, I had my doubts since it came from good old Gramps. I have to admit that I used this method too, but only to impress a naive friend or visitor that stopped to take a few pictures. I even showed this method to an elementary class who came to our farm on a field trip. When I later explained to the adult chaperones that I was joking about the *four buffalo method,* I found out that they were as duped as the little kids.

The buffalo method required two things: a large five-inch kitchen ladle and, of course, a few buffalo. After opening the door to the sugar shack and clearing a visible path, so no one was standing in the doorway, the spoon was dipped and swirled around in the syrup pan. The more dramatic of a swirl, the better, cause this was all about showmanship. Quickly lifting the spoon and holding it horizontal to the horizon at eye level, I would look past the spoon and out the sugar shack door. As the syrup dripped from the spoon, I started counting buffalo as they ran by the door, saying, "One buffalo, two buffalo, three buffalo, four..." As the dripping slowed, the syrup would crystalize on the bottom of the spoon and pull back up. If the syrup stopped dripping when only four buffalo ran by, you had a finished product. The audience was always fixated on the drip of the spoon that they forgot to look for buffalo. I chuckled to myself as I recalled how fun this scene was to play out and how many people enjoyed it.

The actual, more accurate way of testing for readiness was to use a thermometer and a hydrometer. The experts use an expensive refractometer. Syrup is usually done when the boiling temperature of the sap is about seven degrees higher than the 212 degrees it takes for water to boil. To be as accurate as possible, it is also necessary to compensate for the barometric pressure of the day. When the temperature got to about 215 degrees, I switched to using a hydrometer.

This device floats in a one-inch round container of hot syrup. As the sugar content rises, so does the glass hydrometer. The hydrometer has a red line that indicates a scientific and factory-tested classification for the industry standard which verifies that you have syrup.

One more check with the hydrometer showed me the top of the red line; we had reached syrup! The relaxed, easy-going pace quickly changed to a hurry-up offense. If I took too much time, the syrup would go past the desired cooking, and we would get maple candy instead of syrup. Dona and Abe walked in with the stainless-steel, two-gallon pots, and I had the sawhorses already set up for filtering the syrup. Both of us quickly donned leather gloves and gently slid the sugar pan off the firebox and onto the sawhorses. I propped up one end with two bricks and all the syrup ran to the far end of the pan.

By opening the spout on the end of the pan, the 219-degree syrup slowly ran into a filtering container with ten individual filters. As sugar sand clogged up one filter, I pulled it away from the spout and pinned it to the side of the pan. When the stainless-steel pan was three-quarters full, I dumped the filtered syrup into a waiting two-gallon pan with heavy handles. After filtering, everything was carried to the kitchen where the syrup was ladled into sanitized quart jars. Lids and rings were swiftly added so that the hot syrup self-seals the quart jar as it cools. The next day, the quart jars would be transferred to a dark shelf in the cool basement until they were chosen for the table or sold to a friend. Today we capped another nineteen quarts of dark but flavorful Four Buffalo Wisconsin Maple Syrup.

*Love is like wildflowers; it's often found*
*in the most unlikely places. – Ralph Waldo Emerson*

# Wildflowers

Beautiful, Meadow, Wildflowers! Could they be the crown jewel of the essence of creation? With their colors, shapes, delicacy, and beauty, they are indeed a magnum opus! In Wisconsin, we are blessed with a very diverse, unique, and healthy variety of wildflowers. They grow in the woods, the ditches, the sandy knolls, and the backwoods sloughs. Most of them are herbaceous with green, leafy stems that erupt into a blast of color in mid-summer to late fall.

In mid-winter, the once vibrant wildflowers of summer now appear completely dead with dry, gray-brown, brittle stems, but even then, they create a unique and scenic landscape. It is the color in July, August, and September, however, that seems to attract most of us to this gem in nature. And while it may be obvious to others, I have to admit that the fascination of wildflowers, or for that matter any plants in nature, didn't come to my attention early in my young life. I guess I just took them for granted. No, the only plants in nature that came to my attention as a child were the ones that poked and burned and irritated.

One such freak-of-nature plant I discovered very early in my youth had a white, spittle-like substance on its stems. My sisters and I called this foamy substance snake venom because the vicious plant seemed to jump out and bite us when we least expected it. My grandparents' dairy farm had plenty, and it was always in the wrong places.

I remember learning very early in life that stinging nettle, or *burn nettle* as we called it, was something that I needed to identify and to avoid. I discovered burn nettle in all the locations that were fun for a kid. It was around the woodpile, along the barbed-wire fence, and near the junk pile. Granted, these were places we were warned to avoid by the adults, but they were glorious places to find wonderful things to play with. Even the slightest brush against its hairy leaves would leave a burn that seemed to last for an eternity to a ten-year-old. And yes, believe it or not, it's classified as a wildflower and it's edible. It can be used to make a gentle diuretic tea and is used to combat high blood pressure. How in the world can something that creates the pain of death on a child's skin be eaten? Yes, it's a wildflower...no joke!

Another plant that gained my respect early in life was the bull thistle, or *pasture thistle* as we called it. While I knew from looking at it that it was covered in needle-sharp spines and thorns both on its flower and leaves, on the farm one day, I discovered the hard way that it was not a plant I wanted to mess with.

One sunny afternoon, while helping Grandpa bring in the cows for milking, I accidentally stepped in a fresh cow pie out in the meadow. The warm, squishy feeling of a left shoe soaked in olive-green, ripe cow manure had me *pasture-*

*dancing* around on one foot while shaking the other. Losing my balance on a fieldstone after my third or fourth turn, I fell backwards into a thicket of bull thistles.

Grandpa had witnessed the whole scene play out directly in front of him. He quickly rushed to my rescue but didn't quite know which part of me to grab. I was covered in thorns. My face, my arms, my stomach, and my buttocks had all been impaled. He said I looked like a pincushion. He ended up pulling me out by the belt around my britches. I was gingerly and quickly escorted to the barn and stripped down to my tighty-whities.

Grandpa leaned against the doorframe of the milk house and made jokes about city slickers who come to the farm while Grandma, a bit more sympathetic, washed off the cow pie with very cold spring water and pulled out each and every dagger that had impaled my young, delicate body. The nature books say that it's a wildflower too? Are you serious? How on earth can a plant that almost killed a young boy (yes, I thought I was dying) be classified as a wildflower?

With a plethora of poisonous and barbed plants in Wisconsin, it is a wonder why anyone would spend time in the great outdoors. There is wild parsnip and cow parsnip, poison ivy, poison oak, poison hemlock, and field nettles to deal with. There are thistles and barbs and all-out thorns on plants and trees and grasses. Yet, once I got past the precautions of these select few, I found that nature was a glorious, beautiful canvas. There are magnificent trees, flowing grasses, and fragrant blossoms. My favorite, though, seems to be the wildflowers.

Wildflowers come in all sorts of categories. There are color categories and shape categories. There are native plants and invasive plants. There are edible plants and toxic plants. However you categorize them, just don't forget to enjoy them. Yes, even the toxic acid spitting plants from my childhood nightmares are worth this attention and soon drew my curiosity.

As I said before, my enjoyment of wildflowers didn't develop overnight. No, it developed over many years. When I was a child, it was time cutting firewood with my dad or chasing cows with Grandpa; when I was a teenager, it was time I spent deer hunting in my uncle's woods or fishing at the mill pond. But, mostly it was when I spent time as an adult in the fields and woods that I fully gained an appreciation for the wildflower. Some people only see the face value of the plant in its flower. Yet while the flower itself is certainly the gem of the herbaceous plant, I would challenge you to dig a little deeper.

There are many avenues to explore when it comes to the wildflower. The hunt and identification can be the most challenging and, at the same time, the most fun. Discovering where the plant grows and when it blooms may take more than a few visits to the field. In addition, the fun of hunting for wildflowers has several seasons. Summer, of course, is the most popular time to look and identify the wildflowers of our fields and woods. The key is to get out each week because there are different plants flowering throughout the summer months.

If you spend time searching and learning about the magnificent wildflower, you might even become a sleuth-like myth-buster. You might even find yourself defending the reputation of a wildflower. For instance, did you know that the goldenrod wildflower, in all of its brilliant yellow beauty, is not the cause of allergies in late summer like most Sconnies believe? The pollen from goldenrod is too sticky to become airborne. The culprit of most sneezing and headaches is ragweed, not the beautiful goldenrod. The confusion in this myth is that both wildflowers bloom at the same time of year and are often found growing together. With a little investigation and a little education...myth busted, reputation defended!

Besides the wildflower plant itself, there are many other beauties to discover because of them. There are bees and butterflies and hummingbirds that visit the bleach whites, crimson reds, and brilliant yellow wildflowers. These pollinators are attracted to the pollen and nectar of the plant and are hard to miss while you are waist-deep in a bed of asters, columbines, or milkweed. Take along a notepad for observations, a butterfly net for identifying insects, and a few plastic sandwich bags for collecting samples and seeds.

While summer may be the most popular and productive time for wildflower hunting, spring can also be just as entertaining. Early spring is an exhilarating time to be in the outdoors. An advantage in spring is that it is usually void of pesky insects that might detour your day, save a wood tick or two. It's the time of year when everything wakes up. I find it amazing how some plants have buds and can grow out of the ground even before the ground is thawed. Some plants do this by creating their own heat source in the early spring to thaw the ground, which is very advantageous to getting a head start on other plants.

In Wisconsin, this happens about mid to late March. It is usually about the time when we pull the taps from the maple trees. The time when we hear the third sign of spring...the chorus of the frogs. Since Abe and I were already out in the woods collecting and cleaning our sugaring equipment, we usually took a little extra time to see who or what might be poking through the leaves or under some brush in the fence lines. On one such sunny, spring Sunday afternoon was when we met Sunflower.

*Defend the weak, protect both young and old, never desert your friends.*
*Give justice to all, be fearless in battle and always ready*
*to defend the right. – The law of Badger Lords*

# Sunflower

"Man, oh man is the wind blowing today, Abraham," I said as I bent over to pick up a metal pail that had blown off a maple tree and was stuck in a nearby thicket of scarlet hawthorn. "We are going to have to scrub the mud out of this one."

Abe paid no attention to what I was saying, partly because the wind was whistling through the bare tree limbs, creating an eerie howling sound, and partly because his sensitive, black nose had picked up the scent of something. I always found it fascinating to watch Abe working that beautiful, black nose of his. He kept it millimeters from the floor of the woods, but never touched anything with it. It was almost like his nose was in control of his entire body. Indeed, the nose was the master and the body was its slave. Wherever the nose wanted to go, the body always complied. At times, Abe might be in a dead run when his nose told his body to STOP on a dime, make a right turn, and run full-bore again.

As I securely stacked an arm full of metal sap buckets on

the loader of the tractor, I chuckled out loud thinking about watching Abe work that magnificent nose. On one such occasion, while he was just a pup, he had uprooted a wise old cottontail. That experienced old rabbit had Abe running in all kinds of circles, around trees, under a barbed-wire fence, through a stabbing patch of buckthorn, and in and out of tufts of quack grass.

When Abe lost the scent, that old rabbit just watched and waited. Abe would double back and circle and spin, and eventually the chase would start again. If only he had looked up once in a while, he would have discovered that the cottontail was in full view the entire time. But you see, the eyes aren't in control, the nose is! Watching young Abraham that day was very entertaining not only to me, but also to that wise old rabbit. After ten minutes of messing with my dog, Mr. Rabbit finally tired of it and disappeared down into his burrow right where Abe had started the chase. Lesson learned? Hardly.

Today was no different. Spring had sprung, and lots of creatures were out and about today. It was a warm, sunny Sunday afternoon. There was a very good chance that someone would be messing with my poor dog before the day was over. As I put the last buckets in the loader and removed the spiles from my pocket, securing them in the old Folgers coffee can, I hollered at Abe, who was now on the far end of the woods. He looked up at me for a second when he heard my yell, but his nose was in control and he went right back to his exploring.

After a few minutes of impatient waiting, I finally had to walk to him. He was working the very edge of the woods where an old, rusty woven-wire fence had been rolled up, now mostly covered with briars and dead leaves surrounded by fieldstones.

"I'm leaving without you!" I declared as I approached him. There was no response, nothing! He just kept right on circling and sniffing, but a little slower now and with more diligence and refinement.

I was in no hurry to head back to the farm, so I ended up leaning against a young maple tree. My mind began to daydream mindlessly. I was listening to the sounds of spring and chewing on a tasteless, dried stalk of oat grass. As I watched Abe work this leafy piece of wooded real estate, I had a feeling of calm and serenity.

But I was quickly brought back to reality when I saw him suddenly stop. And then I saw him do something that I had never seen him do before. He actually stopped sniffing and lifted his head up! Immediately, he lowered his stance and his ears pulled back. What astonished me is that he looked. For once in his life, he looked up to see what he was stalking. His butt started to wiggle, and I knew he was about to pounce! I was so proud of him that, even though I didn't want any cute bunny to perish, I was hoping that Abe would actually catch something for once. But when I glanced in the direction he was looking and saw what he saw, my relaxed state of mind quickly turned to panic mode.

Cornered between the roll of rusty wire and a pile of fieldstones was an American badger. This was only the second time I had run across a badger in the woods in my fifty-plus years, and, I'm not absolutely sure, but I'm guessing that this was the very first face-to-face encounter with a badger Abe had ever had. Why do I say that, you ask? Two reasons! For one thing, they are rarely seen during the day, and secondly, but more critical to the moment, he was about to pounce on a cornered American BADGER! In my opinion, the badger is one of the fiercest of animals in the woods of Wisconsin, especially when cornered. Why do you think the University of Wisconsin has the badger as its mascot? If Abe had met a badger before, he would know better than to tangle with one.

Understanding that the badger has the toughest reputation in the woods and how they don't back down from a fight, my eyes tripled in size while my anxiety level rose through the roof. Was my young, innocent, fun-loving dog about to tangle with a badger? Seriously?!

Without thinking, I launched my body at Abe, hitting him with a full body slam while yelling at the top of my lungs, "Stop!" He let out a surprised "Yipe!" as all the air was expelled from both his and my lungs. Our bodies hit the ground in a dull thud. I hung on for dear life while trying to get my own breath, Abe was scrambling to get away from whatever monster had just attacked him from behind, and of course, the badger stood her ground.

I soon rolled over into a sitting position and brought my best friend with me. It probably looked pathetic as I hugged his head with both arms, still hanging on as tight as I could. His body was now upside down with all four paws flailing in the wind.

"Uff da, turn him upside right, you is chokin' him 'der hey," a concerned voice said from in front of me.

Yup, you guessed it. It was the badger. For some reason, even though I knew now that some animals could speak, it still surprised me that a wild creature from the deep woods had said something that I understood. I was stunned and could not move. Again, the badger said, "You is chokin' him 'der fa sure by gully, I tells ya!"

I slowly loosened my grip, and Abraham gasped for air and coughed like he had a hair ball stuck in his throat.

"You fair to middlin' 'der hey?" the badger asked.

Abe continued to hack up a lung, sneezed twice, and began licking his upper lip which was now bleeding. "Ok," Abe said, wheezing. "Ok."

All of a sudden, my mind was very fuzzy. While I thought a minute ago that I was doing my dog a favor, saving him from a fierce Tasmanian devil, now I was confused that the rash call to action was interpreted as unnecessary and rude. It took me quite a while to align my thinking with dog and badger. However, after a bit of interaction and conversation with said badger, I eventually caught up to where they were in the woods.

I had just embarrassingly met Sunflower, a stout four-year-old badger that not only lived on the edge of our marsh but was already a very good friend of Abraham's. His *I'm gonna pounce* stance was exactly that. However, he was playing, not fighting. I had read the signs all wrong. I found myself in a position I had never been before in my life, apologizing to a wild Wisconsin American Badger.

Unfortunately, because of my rash call to action, Abe was now limping. His right front paw was badly damaged. It must have been quite painful because he wouldn't let me look at it. He headed toward home without me, limping on the remaining three. I followed behind him, pleading with him to stop, hoping there was some way that I could ease his pain.

"Wait up," I said to Abe as he stumbled over some broken branches.

"Geeez, yoos an idiot 'n so," a voice said from beneath me.

I looked down to see Sunflower quickly huffing along with me step for step.

"I didn't know!" I stammered.

"You pert-neer broke da leg fa sure hey," she fired back.

Frustrated at my own foolishness and concerned that there might be some serious damage, I yelled, "Abe, wait up, let me look at your leg."

When he reached the tractor, Abe finally stopped and sat down to lick his injured black paw. I knelt down beside him, and he let me gently work his tendons and bones.

"Cripes sakes, it's prolly broke 'der hey," a shrill voice said again from behind me.

I looked over my shoulder, still surprised that an American badger was lecturing me. "It's not broke," I softly said as I guided Abe's paw to the ground and patted his head. "Do you want to ride the tractor home?"

"Ya hey 'der now, yoos ain't gunna shoot him, is yoos?" Sunflower sternly bickered.

"No, we ain't gonna shoot him!" I said snidely. "That is something people say about farm horses from the old days. We don't do that anymore."

"Gud, cause I'd take yoos out myself by golly before I'd let ya shoot me friend!" Sunflower declared.

At that, I slowly turned and held my hand out toward Sunflower. "Can we start again?" I asked. "I think we got off on the wrong foot. It's a pleasure to meet you, badger."

"Guldarn, more like da broken foot 'der hey, me, I'm Sunflower," she said as she laid her front left leg on my outstretched hand and gave it a scratch with her very long, sharp claws. "Yoos betcha, now wees even, by golly!"

I got up off my knees and walked to the front of the

tractor. I grabbed the duffel bag that had my lunch in it, sat down in the leaves next to Abe, and leaned against the rear tire of the tractor. I unzipped the canvas bag and pulled out a thermos of cocoa, a sandwich bag of lemon cream sandwich cookies, and a corned beef sandwich that Dona had packed for our lunch.

"Oh by golly 'der, now wees talkin'!" Sunflower declared as I laid half of the sandwich in front of Abe and half at her feet. Abe, still in pain because of his bloody lip and bruised paw, gingerly took a bite. Sunflower, on the other hand, quickly tore the bread off the sandwich and devoured the meat from within. Looking up to see if Abe was going to finish his half, she stood there licking her striped lips. Begrudgingly, she slowly finished off the rest of the sandwich, not very happy with the Thousand Island dressing. I just sat there like a dazed deer in a headlight and watched them both. The cookies didn't last too long either, and I noticed that Abe was now putting weight on his front paw.

I eventually poured a cup of cocoa for myself and was sipping at the hot beverage when out of the blue, Sunflower stood up and said to Abe, "Yoos ok 'der hey? Holy cry-yiy, I gots to get some sleep what-nat." She walked right up and rubbed her head against his head. Then with a swift turn, she scowled at me and waddled off, convinced that Abe was going to live for another day and that I wasn't going to shoot him.

Abe got up, limped over to where I was sitting on the ground, and plopped down with his front legs on my lap. I scrubbed his ears, and we both watched her until she was out of sight. "She's a feisty one!" I said. "I like her."

Abe, after a heavy sigh, softly replied, "Me too."

*I want to think again of dangerous and noble things.*
*I want to be light and frolicsome. I want to be improbable*
*and beautiful and afraid of nothing as though I had wings.*
*– Mary Oliver, "Starlings in Winter"*

# Birds in the Soffit

Abe wanted to walk back to the farm, but I insisted that he ride up on the tractor seat with me. I'm very thankful that he only weighs about forty-two pounds and takes up very little room since there is limited space between the fenders on this David Brown. For most of the ten-minute drive, he lay motionless across my lap with his head under the steering wheel. However, as we transitioned from the dirt path of the field to the gravel driveway of the farm, he rose up onto his front legs. It probably looked a little funny because his head was mostly blocking my view as we attempted to maneuver the bucket of the tractor to stop next to the door of the sugar shack. For some reason, he had to make sure I was doing it correctly, and we struggled with each other for prime viewing. As soon as I shut off the diesel engine, I noticed Ada was perched on her hind haunches behind the barn, stretching her neck to see what was going on. On my second glance, she had disappeared.

Getting an injured dog off the tractor was about as difficult as it had been to get him up there in the first place. I ended up making him sit on the tractor seat until I climbed to the ground, and then he slowly and reluctantly crawled into my arms. He put his front legs over my shoulders, and I reached forward and picked up his stiff body by the back legs. I sat him on the ground as gingerly as I could maneuver a 42-pound sack of feed...I mean black, hairy dog. As I turned around toward the front of the tractor, I almost stepped on you-know-who. It startled me to see a large, brown woodchuck beneath my feet still working on a dandelion blossom.

"You could warn a guy!" I stammered.

"What happened to him?" Ada asked with her mouth full.

"We had a little mishap in the woods. His front paw has a sprain," I replied. "He'll survive."

"The Mrs. is looking for you. She even walked behind the barn to see if you were out back."

"Do you know what she wants?" I asked.

"Nope, she don't talk to me." And with that, she waddled back behind the barn, convinced that there was nothing further to investigate.

No sooner had we unloaded the tractor than the Mrs. was calling from the back porch. I couldn't hear what she was saying, so I motioned with my hand and hollered that we would be there in a couple minutes.

Abe was able to hobble up the back three steps all by himself, although a little slower than usual. I stopped on the porch to remove my muddy boots, and then we both walked into the kitchen together. To my surprise, we were met by an agitated woman with a broom handle in her hand. The sweeping head of the broom had been removed, and she stood there with just the wooden handle in both hands and a frustrated look on her face.

"Dare I ask what you are doing with a broom handle?" I inquired.

"Either those starlings go or I go!" she blurted.

"Come again?"

"Follow me!" she grunted as she brushed past us and headed up the stairs.

Abe was not interested and slowly made his way to his bed by the woodstove. I, however, did not have the luxury of ignoring the wife, so I curiously followed her up the stairs.

As I sheepishly tagged along behind her, my brain struggled with this mystery I was presented with. I have seen the Mrs. angry many times, but never while holding a broom handle. I guess it could be worse. She could be after me with the broom, but it was obvious that I was not the focus of her need to bear arms. For the life of me, though, I had no idea what she was up to.

The upstairs of our country farmhouse was fairly straightforward. The stairs led to a central fifteen-by-ten room, actually more of a very wide hallway, that then split off into four separate rooms. All of them were bedrooms except one, and that was where we were headed. This was a room where the door was always open unless it was occupied. It surprised me to see the door closed and her hand on the doorknob. "Get ready," she said. And she quietly and slowly opened the bathroom door.

As soon as the door opened, I heard a muffled and confusing sound. The bathroom window was open, and the window screen had been removed and was currently leaning against the bathtub. She stepped aside and pointed out the window. I just stood there with a stupid look on my face while my brain failed to compute. After some heated, one-sided conversation, I was informed that she had spent most of the morning fighting with a bird that wanted to nest in the soffit of our house. The broom handle was her choice of hardware to fight this battle, and clearly it was not working, but I will let you tell her that. I was not about to add fuel to the fire.

The upstairs bathroom was built into the roof of our house so that the edge of the walls followed the contour of the roof. Next to the toilet was a small two-foot-long, one-foot-high sliding window. Directly outside this window was the edge of our roof on the east side of our house. The previous owner had the old, faded wood trim of the house wrapped in aluminum, and downspouts had been added. However, this was hastily installed and had left small gaps in the aluminum soffit. These small gaps had attracted a pair of starlings. They had proceeded to peel back an opening wide enough for entry, and I could see small sticks in the cracks of the soffit.

I assured Dona that this was causing no harm to the house, but she reasserted that either they were going to be evicted or she was leaving. While I highly doubted that she was ready to leave me and the kids over a pair of lovebirds, I did not attempt to call her bluff. I simply and gently assured her that I would take care of the problem. How hard could it be to evict a pair of simple birds and fix the hole in the soffit anyway? Piece of cake! Right?

I should probably save you my frustration, but I was impressed with the tenacity and engineering skills of this mating pair of starlings, not to mention the determination to keep their home intact. Let me just say that a ladder did not help deter this starling couple. In fact, as soon as I leaned the ladder against the house, they started swooping my head and almost caused me to fall when my foot missed a rung of the ladder while I swung at them with my hat.

After several minutes of aviation terror, I was able to make my way to the top of the ladder and peek inside the hole they had made. Sure enough, there was a very impressive nest built in our soffit. It was constructed of locust branches, which are tough but pliable. I could see green leaves and grass lining the inside and feathers and string throughout. This was not your average robin's nest. No, this was a massive, engineered, architectural masterpiece. It looked like the entire four feet of soffit was packed full of nesting material. This was not going to be easy.

What I thought was going to be a simple ten-minute job ended up taking the better part of two hours. After removing all the nails that held the soffit in place, I pried open a slot along the entire four-foot section. I ended up working back in the bathroom and hanging out the small opening. Using my wife's broom handle, I was able to slide the building material out the end and onto the ground two stories below. But, to my surprise, there were more than two starlings in our soffit.

As soon as the nesting material hit the ground, I saw a flurry of activity. There were wings everywhere. Besides Mom and Dad, three other adult starling pairs had joined the battle, and it quickly became obvious what all the fuss was about. I ran downstairs and around the front of the house to find four fuzzy baby birds crawling across the lawn. Mom and Dad had been busy up in that soffit, and they had been in there longer than we knew. They already had a family, a family of four of the cutest little birds I'd ever seen. My heart sank. I had just evicted an entire family. How could I be so insensitive and cruel. To add to my dismay, I glanced up at the first-floor dining room window to see Abraham watching it all. He let out a shrill bark, and I thought for a second that I saw him shaking his head back and forth in disapproval.

My brain was instantly working on a solution. As the gears turned in my head, Abe let out another bark and a light bulb turned on in all that gray matter. Hey, we had a large box elder tree on the south side of our house that was full of starling families. This tree was so riddled with holes that we had seen a plethora of wildlife come and go from that tree over the years. Earlier this spring, I had seen a male wood duck show his mate this tree as a potential nesting site. I quickly moved the ladder from the east side of the house to the box elder tree and picked up most of the nesting material. I shoved it into the lowest hole on the tree and caught all four of the starlets while the parents and their sadistic friends attempted to pluck my eyes out and remove all the hair from my head. I put all four baby birds in the new nest, and their mom and dad quickly came to their rescue.

We would have to keep a close eye on this nest from the kitchen window for a few days just to be sure, but within minutes, it looked like this solution was going to work. I was proud of the parents who quickly took to their new home. The dad soon began collecting building materials from the litter that fell from the soffit to renovate what the moving company had hastily assembled as a nest, while the momma completely rearranged every stick in the cavity of the tree. It may not have been the real estate of choice, but it seemed that even with birds, home is where your family is.

*You have to get beyond your*
*own precious inner experiences. – Stella Adler*

# Stella

The next morning, Abe promptly had me up at 6:17am as usual. However, as I half-consciously made my way downstairs, I sensed that something was missing in his normal morning routine. All of a sudden, it came to my attention that he was not ringing the sleigh bells at the back door. I stopped about halfway down the stairs and listened for a moment, but there was no sound coming from the kitchen except the tick-tock of Grandma's old cuckoo clock that hung by the pantry door.

I continued down the last seven steps and rounded the corner. Sure enough, the bells were undisturbed, and Abe was missing. Yawning and rubbing a couple crispies out of my eye socket, I stopped in the doorframe of the stairwell to look across the kitchen for Abe, thinking maybe one of the kids had left a late-night snack in his food bowl and he was making the withdrawal. Nope, he wasn't at his food bowl either. Scanning the room further, I found him with his front paws up on the kitchen sink. He was tilting his head sideways and back and forth like a dog does when it is confused about something. He was listening by the window over the sink, but he wasn't tall enough to look outside. I shuffled over to the coffeepot and plugged it in, and then I joined him at the sink and rested my hand on the back of his neck.

"What ya listening to?" I asked while I yawned a second time and looked out the window.

"Bird," he said.

I couldn't hear anything, and I still couldn't focus very well as my eyes attempted to adjust to the bright light of the sun coming through the window. After another crispy was removed, I took a second glance out the window and noticed that there was a major commotion out by the box elder tree. Our three cats, Norman, Sam, and Gimli, had the tree surrounded like a pride of lions ready to make a kill in the plains of Africa. At the base of the tree was one of the four baby starlets. Mom and Dad were in a frenzy along with many other adult starlings who were dive-bombing the felines. The attempt to deter the pride was not working.

"Let's go rescue her," I said as I stumbled to the back door and quickly slipped into a pair of mud boots.

As I opened the porch door, I realized that Abe's sprained foot was all healed up. He flew past me and down the outside steps in one giant leap, proving that all systems were a go. Within seconds, he was circling the pride of lions. He swiftly chased away the threatening enemy and secured the perimeter. However, now the attention was turned on him as the flock of angry starlings chased him with the intent to kill. One continually pecked him on the head while three others plucked the hairs from his heinie. Poor guy, he ran in circles with his tail tucked until they drove him right in through the open barn door. Ada just so happened to be sitting in front of the barn door watching the whole commotion and was pummeled in the process. Now, not only the good Samaritan, but the innocent bystander became a victim of this hate crime. There was black and brown fur flying everywhere mixed in with a few stray feathers.

I quickly took advantage of the strategic distraction that Abe had created and rescued the starlet from the ground. I shimmied up the tree, with baby in tow, just far enough to reach up to the nest. As I stretched up over my head into the nest, I could feel the warmth of the other brothers and sisters, so I quickly placed the baby in the middle and dropped to the ground. As I did, the mess down by the barn was headed my way. Ada was hightailing it around the south corner, headed for the safety of her rotten log, while two starlings kept her moving. Abe and three other birds were headed for the back door of the house. By the time I got to Abe's rescue, he was scratching at the door to get in. He had had enough! His gracious attempt to help the starlings had not been received as it was intended.

Once we were safely inside, Abe went to licking his wounds and I poured a cup of coffee and moved to the sink window. "Wow, Abe, that was extreme!" I proclaimed as I looked up to the nest in the tree while taking a sip. Almost choking, I immediately said, "Oh dear, here we go again!"

That little starlet had flown the coop again! The cats were already watching and waiting. If I didn't act quickly, its doom was imminent. This time, I donned a hooded sweatshirt and left Abe in the house. I rushed to the garage and grabbed the stepladder. As I approached the tree, the cats backed off, but the war of birds began. This time, I took a little more time to make sure this baby would stay in the tree. By the time I had her safe and sound, I had been hit with at least a dozen blows to the head and hands. "Good parents," I thought to myself. "I would be doing the same thing if someone attacked my family." Leaving the ladder where it was, I ran for the house.

As I came through the back door, I saw Abe up at the kitchen sink again. He turned to look at me and simply said, "Try again!" I skirted to the window to find the exact scene as before. Baby bird on the ground, cats in pounce mode, terrorized parents doing aerial acrobatics. Ugh!

"Oh crap, I'll be right back," I said.

This time, I did not return her to the nest. I picked her up and placed her in the front pocket of my sweatshirt and walked back to the house with birds and cats in tow. Getting in the door without the unwanted company that was following me ended up being more of a challenge than I expected. Abe watched from the porch window while I kicked at the cats and swatted at the birds. Eventually, I was able to close the porch door to leave the cats and starlings to settle things amongst themselves. Walking into the kitchen from the porch, I gently extracted our little friend from my front pocket.

"What do we name this one, Abe?" I asked softy.

Since most creatures who impacted our lives on the farm had names, it only seemed proper that this little gal get one too. I started listing out loud all the female names I could think of that began with ST for starling...I surprised myself at how short that list was. "Stacey, Stephanie, Storm, Stella. Yeah, how about Stella?!" I glanced down at Abe, who was sitting at my feet looking up at the baby starling. "What do you say we name her Stella?" I asked. At the wag of the tail I met approval. "Stella it is then," I declared.

I dug through the recycling container, with Abe's help of course, and found a cardboard box. Then Abe brought me a couple yellow work gloves from the cedar crate, and we made a little cloth nest for her in the bottom of the box. I cautiously placed her in the man-dog nest, but immediately, she jumped out and attempted to remove herself from the box.

"What are we going to do with her?" I asked. "She is going to be trouble." This would later turn out to be a prophetic statement.

With a little ingenuity, advice from gabby Ada, and the search and destroy nose of Abe, we had a new home ready for Stella by lunchtime. Abe discovered an old wire cage in the barn that we had used to house a pet rabbit named Sunshine, and Ada recommended adding some branches to simulate a real nest. We then lined the bottom with newspaper and added a small pocket mirror we stole from the wife's purse. Stella immediately took to the branches and seemed to like her friend in the mirror. Our next challenge was how to feed and water this baby.

"Internet," I said out loud. "Let's see who else has done this before."

Sure enough, we found all the information we needed on the World Wide Web. Surprisingly, scrambled eggs ended up being her favorite food, and she learned to drink her own water within the day. We also learned that starlings make great house pets, but that idea was quickly shot down by the lady of the house. We did gain a little time with the Mrs., however, when she allowed us to put Stella's new home on a shelf next to the west kitchen window. That way, Stella would have the companionship of Mom and Dad through the window screen until she was a few days older and wiser. At least this would be a safe haven from the lion pride!

So that was how we met Stella. She had a very full life already. In the first dozen days of her life, she had been evicted from the soffit, jumped ship, and had been rescued three times! What would be next in her exciting, trouble-filled life I wondered?

*Goodbye? Oh no, please can't we go*
*to page one and do it all over again? – Winnie the Pooh*

# Flown the Coop

The next few weeks ended up being a lot of fun and, at the same time, quite a bit of hard work. Baby birds need a lot of attention, and we wanted to make sure Stella was going to thrive. After a few days of trial and error, we had developed a routine that worked for us and kept her content, well, as content as a wild bird can be in a wire cage in the kitchen.

The first thing in this routine was that Abe and I added scrambled eggs, hold the butter and salt, to our morning schedule. Four eggs, three for me and one for Stella. Abe eventually worked us up to five eggs so he could join the breakfast buffet also. Stella, excited and restlessly fluttering around in her cage, would sometimes spill her water dish while I hurried to get her eggs cooled off each morning.

"I'll add a teaspoon of grape jelly if you behave," I would tease.

Abe would interject, "Me too."

"Dogs don't like grape jelly," I would reply, which was followed by the head laid on the floor and the sad puppy-dog eyes looking up at me. "Ok, but you better eat it." Followed by tail wagging again!

Next on the schedule was a cage cleaning. This was about as chaotic as it got. Stella would fly around her cage in a frenzy as old newspaper was removed and new paper was installed. Abe even added a bark once in a while. We always put the comics on top so she could entertain herself, and we noticed that she liked to poop on the politicians. When things settled down, we would move a few sticks in the cage so her perch was a bit different every day. We quickly learned that cleaning her pocket mirror was very important and made Stella very happy. The bird in the mirror was like making a new friend each day for her. She spent many hours head bobbing and singing to her friend.

When she was very young, we fed her every two hours with high-protein foods, but eventually her appetite settled down so that we fed her only two times a day. Eggs, as I said, were the morning favorite. Ada got into the mix by finding a few garden grubs once in a while, which were added to Stella's evening diet along with a few grapes cut in half, lettuce leaves, and applesauce. She became spoiled early on and would turn up her nose to any store-bought bird food options. For Stella, it had to be homemade.

Sticking to the routine was very important to Stella. Like a lot of females, when she was hungry, she let you know. I learned to ignore her, but Abraham couldn't take her incessant squawking. If he couldn't get outside to avoid the noise, he would find whoever was available inside the house and nudge them with his nose several times. Ringing the bells was his last resort to gather attention.

But no matter how irritated Abraham seemed to get, you

had better not come between the two of them. He became very protective of his bird Stella. It was almost like he became her surrogate mother. He sat for hours next to her cage, watching her. He would often fall asleep on the cold linoleum kitchen floor instead of the warmth of his soft dog pillow by the woodstove just to comfort her.

If anyone came in the back door, he would run to her cage and stand between them and her, heading off any harm that might come her way. And those cats had better keep their distance! Before Stella came into our lives, Abe used to tolerate the farm cats with all their quirky antics, but now he constantly chased them all the way down to the barn or under the old granary to keep them far away from the back steps. He was not about to let them anywhere near his baby bird. And then one day, it happened! We knew it was coming. I guess it was inevitable.

While cleaning Stella's cage one Saturday morning, I accidentally left her cage door open on my way to get clean newspaper from the back porch. I no more than opened the back door when she flew right by my head, out the door, and clean out of sight. Abe barked and took out my legs as he flew through the door after her. I fell into the bag of cat food and spilled the recycling container on my way to the porch floor, catching my chin on the crate of work gloves. Stunned as I was, I instantly knew that Stella was gone. She had literally flown the coop! Within minutes, Abe returned, out of breath, with his tongue hanging out of his mouth and head hanging low. He had lost his baby girl.

*Ain't no thing like me, except me!*
*– Rocket (Guardians of the Galaxy)*

# The Orphans

The next few mornings were spent walking the grounds and calling for Stella. I'm sure we looked fairly pathetic as we moved about the farm. Abraham led the way with his master close behind. Bringing up the rear was Ada jabbering endlessly. Abe would scope out all the nooks and crannies, looking down every hole in the barnyard and under every bush. A bit more realistic, I kept my eyes to the sky and called out her name every few minutes, throwing in a whistle or two. Ada on the other hand just dished out advice to Abe and me while she hopped along behind us.

"Maybe you shouldn't have left her door open," she declared.

"Ya think?" I sarcastically replied.

"She is probably starving to death out in the wild, the poor baby, if she hasn't been plucked like a Sunday chicken by our resident paragon falcon or some other wild animal."

"Like you?" I snapped.

"Very funny. I was talking about those raccoons that have infested your barn."

"The what?"

"The raccoons in your barn," she said a second time as she stood on her hind feet to watch Abe flush out a couple mourning doves from under a blue spruce.

"She's not here, Abe. Let's go look in the barn."

Abe didn't follow right away, and Ada was busy trying to collapse a stalk in the garden for her morning breakfast. I was left to investigate the barn by myself. It was now late June, and the mulberry trees were just starting to produce berries. If there were raccoons in the barn, this would be the time of year that they would be in there.

Most years, I would know that the mulberries were ripe on the trees because the baby raccoons, called cubs or kits, would fill the trees and bicker with each other over what part of the tree was their own personal property, unwilling to share it with their siblings. This usually happened about two o'clock in the morning. Since we slept with our windows open, due to the lack of an air conditioning unit, this was something that I was privileged to enjoy on a lot of humid midsummer nights. Most of the family could sleep right through the racket in the front yard, but not this light sleeper. I would lay in my soft, comfortable bed for hours, listening to the screams and chirps of these fighting kids. It often reminded me of my own family and the squabbles that developed over the silliest things in life, like who's toy it was, who had it first, and why sharing was not an option.

As I opened the haymow door, it was pretty obvious that Ada was correct. We indeed had someone living in the barn. There were droppings everywhere, and they had not been there a week ago. As I stood in the doorway with my hands on my hips, I felt Abe brush past me and immediately start to growl.

"Good Lord, Abe, it looks like we have an infestation. You thinking possum or coon?"

Abe didn't respond with words as usual. He had his nose to the barn boards and began snorting and sneezing as he attempted to get the scent. I stood in the doorway and watched my dog work that beautiful nose. He began zigzagging all over the empty hayloft floor. I'm sure he had a system of navigation to cover every inch of questionable crime scene, but I couldn't figure out his pattern. Most certainly the nose was in charge of his body again, taking him back and forth and around and over and under and sometimes right into things.

After a few minutes, he moved his investigation to the second layer of the haymow. Since we didn't have any farm animals anymore, we had built a couple workshops inside the haymow, or hayloft as some people call it. One room had been intended to house the exercise equipment for the Mrs., but since the treadmill and weight machine weren't getting used in the basement of the house, I couldn't see how it would ever be used in the upstairs of a dairy barn.

One shop room was for woodworking, and one was used for chainsaw sharpening and storing tools for the lawn mower and vehicles. Both of the shop rooms were insulated and had electric heat so I could work comfortably in the wintertime. The hayloft had a roof about thirty feet above the floor, so we had built a ceiling on each room that was nine feet tall. This allowed for a second level in the hayloft where anything and everything was stored. Things like maple syrup pans and buckets, old broken chairs, camping equipment, and empty boxes from computers and household equipment were all piled up above the shop rooms. We had built wooden stairs up to the second level, and Abe's nose, as I stated, was already leading him up those stairs.

As he slowly shuffled up the stairs, I could see the hair raised up on his back. I followed him and let him work for a few minutes.

"You getting close?" I asked.

There was no reply from him at first, but all of a sudden, he stopped in the middle of the shop ceiling and scratched at the wood beneath his feet. I thought it very strange that he stopped at that point. Was he after a chipmunk or mouse in the ceiling of the shop? I started walking toward him.

Just as I reached the top of the stairs, I stopped dead in my tracks. Peeking up from the barn wall about five feet from Abraham was a raccoon cub with jet black eyes and the cutest mask I've ever seen. Abe was still busy working in the middle of floor. If he would have looked up, he would have realized that he was less than five feet from a real live raccoon. But his nose was in control of his body, and it was occupied with the middle of the floor.

I was just about to inform him that he was being watched when he began to pounce on the floor with all four feet. He jumped straight up and hit the floor with all of his weight, doing it again and again and again. After his tenth or eleventh jump, I thought I had better investigate. By now, the baby raccoon was nowhere in sight, having disappeared down the wall of the hayloft.

"What on earth are you doing?" I questioned. "Are you trying to break the ceiling of the shop? Is there something IN the shop?"

At that, Abe immediately stopped, looked up at me, and ran down the stairs, stopping at the closed woodshop door. I hurried down the stairs after him to see him standing point at the door like an English Setter.

"Is something in the shop?" I repeated.

As I reached for the shop door handle, he crouched a bit and started growling again. I intended to sneak into the room quietly, but Abe pushed the door wide open as soon as I turned the handle. It was pitch black in the room, which made no difference to Abraham. Before I could reach for the light switch, I heard what sounded like World War III. There was excited barking, things crashing, and equipment breaking. When the light finally lit the room, all I could see was a cloud of sawdust throughout the room. Abe was after something that was very fast and agile. No, two things... no three...wait...four young raccoons were tearing my woodshop to shreds with Abe trying to follow their every move. After what seemed like forever, all four of the little rascals found a large hole in the drywall behind the table saw and scooted up the wall, across the ceiling, down the stairs, and out the barn door behind me. Abe stopped at the hole in the shop wall and barked continually.

"Those little terrors from hell!" I stammered. "They chewed a hole in our brand-new drywall. What a mess! We have an infestation indeed. They have got to go!" At that, Abe barked one last time as if to say he completely agreed with my every word.

*As soon as I saw you, I knew an adventure
was going to happen. – Winnie the Pooh*

# Adoption

"What a mess, Abe!" I complained as I investigated the large hole that had been excavated in my shop wall. The eight-inch fiberglass insulation was pulled out and scattered on the shop floor along with chewed-up pieces of sheet rock. I was concerned about the electrical wiring that was now exposed. Running my hand along the 12-2 yellow electrical wire, I discovered that the raccoons had worked around the wire without chewing any pieces out of it. Rethinking my technique, I guess it was lucky for my bare hands and my fifty-plus heart that I did not find any bare wires. "Let's find a broom," I said as I headed out the door.

It went without saying that Abe was much more agile and much quicker than I was. By the time I reached the utility shed, aka the bottom of the dairy barn, he was already dragging out the push broom by its bristles. In addition to the broom, I grabbed a garbage can and scoop shovel. As we turned to head back to the hayloft, I heard the gentle voice of Ada beneath my feet.

"Told ya," she said.

"Yup, you were correct as usual, Ada. Please don't tell me that they are friends of yours because they are not living in my barn."

"But they are orphans. They have no place to go," she replied.

"Orphans? Are you sure? They looked pretty healthy to me. You sure that their momma isn't around somewhere?"

"Remember that gunshot a couple days ago about midnight from the neighbor's farm? That was Momma getting caught in the chicken coop."

"How do you know these things? No, I do not remember hearing a gunshot about midnight." I replied, astonished that a woodchuck could tell time and know everybody's business in the whole neighborhood.

"Sunflower, your archnemesis, told me," Ada quipped.

"You know about Sunflower too? Is there no privacy on this farm?"

"Your business is my business. Quit avoiding my question. What about the orphans?"

Just then, we reached the hayloft door. As the three of us walked to the shop, we heard a scampering up the shop wall and the pitter-patter of feet across the ceiling. Abe turned abruptly to run up the stairs and plowed into Ada, who was standing on her hind feet in an attempt to see above the shop. Surprised and bruised, Ada ran out the door and headed to her log behind the barn. Abe paused for a moment to regain his composure, which provided me an opportunity to call off the attack.

"Better let them be, Abe. Sounds like we have to think this through."

After twenty minutes of cleanup, we decided to leave everything right there in the shop, expecting another episode of raccoon mischief in the very near future.

"Maybe I'm thinking about this all wrong. Maybe these orphans need to be relocated, not just evicted. Maybe I am out of my league here. Maybe I don't know what to do. Any suggestions?"

At that, Abe scooted out the hayloft door and headed behind the barn in a hurried trot. "Where are you going?" I yelled. "Am I supposed to follow you?" There was no reply, and he was quickly out of earshot.

I decided that I had better find out what he was up to. Concerned that he was still in hot pursuit of four terribly cute raccoon cubs, I hurried around the corner of the barn to see Abe jump over a log near Ada's den and disappear into the woods. He was on a mission about something.

I started walking down the road that led to the "back forty" grove of maple trees and called for Abe a few times. As I glanced back toward the farm, I saw Ada sitting on her log, watching me. When I turned back around, I could see something at the end of the road, no, two things, one behind the other, and they were headed my way.

Within seconds, I recognized Abe, but there was something strange about his form. I could tell that he was in a hurry, but whoever was following behind him was struggling to keep up. Abe would trot a few yards, stop, and turn around and wait. Trot a few yards, stop, and turn around and wait. It was quite comical, so I just stopped where I was and watched.

As the posse got close, I thought there was a skunk following Abe, but soon I recognized that the striped black-and-white body was Sunflower. With her short legs, she was struggling to keep up with Abe, and I could hear her jabbering about something in the same stern voice she had scolded me with a few weeks before. By the time they reached me, Sunflower was out of breath.

"Good morning, Sunflower," I said. "What are you two characters up to?"

It took a few minutes for Sunflower to reply since she was wheezing like a heavy smoker. This pause in the action allowed Ada to catch up to the group. Never in my life could I have imagined that I was about to have a four-way conversation with my dog, a woodchuck, and a badger.

"What's going on?" Ada interrupted.

"By gully I tells ya, Abe said sometin bout 'der rescue hey?" Sunflower finally gasped.

"You…" I started saying before being cut off.

"You talking about the orphans?" Ada interjected. "Is that what this is all about Abe? Yeah, Sunflower, those baby raccoons moved into the hayloft of his barn. Remember you told me that the momma got caught in the neighbor's hen house?"

"Cripes sakes the poor ting, she was jist trying to borrow dem a few eggs to feed da kids once 'der hey," Sunflower replied. "Da farm rat splained me dat she took on dat der blue-tick all by herzself by gully, long enough ainna her babes git away. She'd a made it too if dat flea bag weren't so blasted loud, I tells ya. All dat der noise wokes up da boss, and he dispatched gud al ma with da scatter gun. Fee-da, I spose dis guy is gunna shoot em 'der orphans too, ainna he? I tink Abe splain me to stop him 'der hey?"

"You sure got me pegged all wrong, Sunflower," I snapped. "While I don't appreciate the mess in my barn, I am not a cold-hearted exterminator. I think the rescue Abe is asking for is a relocation, someplace a little more natural for them to grow up."

"Bingo," Abe interjected in his many words of explanation.

"Uff da," Sunflower blurted. "She's da famly o' four, ain't she?"

"Yup, you got it!" Ada said, taking the words out of my mouth.

Since Abe and I were just flies on the wall in the conversation, I squatted down next to him and plucked a blade of grass to chew on while the two ladies sorted out the details. Now I understood why Abe only said one-word phrases. It wasn't that he couldn't complete a full sentence, it's that it was hard to get a word in edgewise around these two beautiful gabby girls.

After a half hour of brainstorming, it was decided that Sunflower would talk to an old raccoon in the hollowed-out maple in the marsh past the maple grove. Evidently, this old coon had a matriarchal reputation and several vacant rooms in her holy tree. Sunflower thought this old dame would be a perfect mentor for the four orphans. This experienced old coon, named Bella, was known as a very strict, but wise and caring, grandma raccoon. With everyone in agreement, Sunflower headed off to the marsh and the rest of us headed back to the farmstead.

That same night at dusk, while the Mrs. and I sat in our rocking chairs on the back porch, enjoying the fiery red and orange sunset while sipping on brandy old-fashioneds, I noticed Abe's ears perk up when he lifted his head off the wooden porch floor. Squinting through the shadows, I caught a glimpse of a large, gray raccoon leading four young cubs through the barnyard and down the tractor path. They were headed to the marsh.

"Good rescue, Abe!" I said as I reached down and patted him on the head. "Good rescue!"

With the twitch of the tail, I could tell that he felt as proud as me. Even though raccoons were not our favorite animals on the farm, it felt peaceful to know that the orphans had been adopted. A smile came across my face as I leaned back in my rocking chair and took another sip of brandy.

*Diamonds are a girl's best friend, and dogs are a man's best friend.*
*Now you know which sex has more sense.*
*– Zsa Zsa Gabor*

# Time for Bed

For Abe, most days ended before the ten o'clock TV news. About 9:15pm, Abe would usually come over to my recliner and lay his heavy, hairy head on my lap. It was his way of telling me it was not just time for bed, it was time for sleep. I'm sure if you asked him, he would explain that his bed by the woodstove, while very comfortable, was nothing like the soft, fluffy comforter on the master's bed. At the end of his day, he looked forward to this one simple gratification. He usually nudged me to go to bed as early as possible, not necessarily because he was tired, but because he had learned that his pleasure on the end of the master's bed would be short-lived. While I enjoyed letting Abe sleep at the foot of my bed, the wife did not. In fact, as soon as the Mrs. came to bed, usually twenty minutes later, Abe would be banished to his upstairs dog pillow on the floor out in the hallway.

The scene would play out something like this. Immediately when Dona started to walk up the stairs, Abe would give a moan as if to say, "Oh great...here comes trouble." When Dona would eventually walk into the bedroom after a bathroom stop and checking on the kids, Abe's eyes would watch her every move. His body remained perfectly still, and his head would not move from laying across my ankles. I think he thought that if he acted like a statue, she might not notice he was there. Would this be the night that he would get to secretly spend the entire night on the plush, quilted, warm blankie at the end of the master's bed? If all the stars lined up just right, once in a blue moon, he would be permitted to stay.

Unfortunately, he was seldom authorized to linger more than just a few short minutes each night. Dog hair on the bed was the wife's excuse, but I'm pretty sure her reasoning was a bit more personal. I'll admit that Abe's fine, black hair seemed to be everywhere in the house, but that was what vacuum cleaners and wash machines were for, right? If a vacuum cleaner was going to cause nervous frustration to each and every dog in the world, it might as well be used for something good, don't you think?

Well, after several years of the same old circus act between dog and lady of the house, Abe concluded that she had an alternative motive. He was pretty sure the dog hair was just an excuse she complained about to make sure she got her man to herself for a few hours each and every night. She was just plain jealous, according to Abe. She was jealous that he was always by my side, inside the house, outside the house, in the car, in the woods, and in the barn. Apparently, she thought that the master had more meaningful conversations with the dog than with her, the wife, the "best friend" of thirty years. Yup, that's right, according to Abe, she had dog envy!

There was another theory floating around, however. It

could also be that she didn't like the fact that Abe was very good at creeping up higher and higher on the bed during the night. Once the humans were sound asleep, he never seemed to stay at the end of the bed.

When Abe was a puppy, I would often let him sleep at the end of our bed so he didn't whimper and whine during the night. I tried everything, including putting my daily t-shirt in his kennel for security, but nothing seemed to stop his incessant whining unless he was immediately by my side, on my lap or on my bed. Finally, he trained me to put a special blanket at the end of the bed as the cure. The problem with that was that we would often wake up to find him in the center of the bed between us, with his head on a pillow, legs stretched out, and both of us hugging opposite edges of the bed, barely hanging on, while the dog enjoyed the soft, warm sweet spot of the bed.

As the months dragged on, Abe became the quote and we ended up as mere quotation marks on the outer edges of the bed. This all seemed to come to a head when Dona woke up one morning cheek to beak with Abraham. Soon after dog drool started appearing on her pillow, she started banishing him not only to his pillow on the floor, but to his pillow moved out into the hallway. Reluctant as he was, Abe quickly realized that he, the simple peasant, was subject to the edict of the Queen.

In time, however, Abe eventually adopted a positive attitude about it all, that sleeping in the hallway was actually a good location to spend the night. It was a great vantage point to keep an eye on the entire family all at once. He was placed at the top of the stairs just outside all three upstairs bedrooms. This unique location allowed him to monitor everyone at once and no longer hold back on dog farts. But even though he had now found contentment in the hallway, this didn't stop him from jumping on the master's bed each and every night and groaning when the Queen pointed to the door.

Tonight, as Abe came over to my recliner, I told him he had to wait for the weather report before we could head upstairs. Earlier in the day, Ada had mentioned that she could feel weather coming our way, so I wanted to see if the weatherman agreed. Sure enough, according to the meteorologist on TV, thunderstorms were headed our way sometime after midnight. Once again, Ada the furry "prophet" was correct.

So, as the teeth were brushed and the sleeping kids were tucked in, Abe waited patiently next to the bed until I climbed in. Just as he vaulted up on the bed, I reached down and patted his head. "It's going to be a long night for you, old man," I said. I'm not sure he fully understood me because he cocked his head sideways like dogs do when they are trying to figure something out, but the peasant laid his hairy head down across my left ankle and closed his eyes to enjoy the few precious minutes of the day before the Queen came to bed.

*Many the morn when the mist covers the valley as I softly call,*
*'Come, Boss, come, Boss,' and the day begins with a shining promise*
*of fresh milk and churned butter on the table.*
*– Donald Abrams, 1924*

# Cows are Out

It seemed as though my eyes had barely closed when I was awakened by lightning flashes through my eyelids. At first, they were few and far between, but within minutes, the flashes were almost continual with rolling thunder sounding louder and closer. I started counting the seconds between lightning and thunder, but the frequency made the calculations difficult. Adding to my awakening was Abraham sitting next to the side of my bed with the most pathetic, saddest whimper I had ever heard.

"Get up here," I sleepily murmured.

Before I had finished my sentence, I could feel the pressure of his body on my legs with his head burrowing under the extra blanket at the end of the bed. "You big baby," I declared as I sat up to give him a reassuring pat on the butt.

Needless to say, Abraham did not like thunder. There was something about the percussion of loud noises that hurt him to his core. Fourth of July was the absolute worst. Gunshots and loud trucks were almost as bad. Hunting dog, he was not!

Almost any noise that simulated thunder would drive him to take cover between your legs, behind the couch, or under the bed. He seemed to be the most content if he could hide while pressing up against a friend. If there was a loud burst of noise heard while you were sipping on your coffee, you had less than a second to secure your hot cup of joe before Abe and all of his forty-two pounds would be up on your lap with his head tucked under your arm.

I had no more than finished getting Abe settled on the bed when both lightning and thunder shook the entire house at the same time. The flash lit up the bedroom like someone was arc welding right there in the room. The thunder rocked the house until I thought the windows were going to burst. The impulse of spontaneous surprise caused both husband and wife to grab each other out of fear and panic with Abe sandwiched in between. Abe was now burrowing deeper into the bed, and we could hear the stomping of little feet from the hallway. The door suddenly crashed open, and three kids body-slammed my wife just as frightened as Abraham. Immediately, there was another flash followed by a deafening crash of thunder.

"Holy cow! That was close," I blurted.

"You better go check the other kids," the wife fired back. "And close all the windows too."

As I climbed out of bed, wondering why I was the lucky one to secure the house, I thought about taking my dog with me. However, he was now lost in the mix of arms and legs that were scrambling to get under the covers. I could hear the waves of rain hitting the vinyl siding of the house and quickly stumbled from room to room, checking windows and remaining kids. To my astonishment, I found the oldest boy sound asleep. "How is that even possible?" I asked myself as I checked to make sure he was still breathing, as parents often do, and headed back to bed.

The power had already gone out, so once the house was deemed secure, I located a flashlight and a box of matches for the bedroom candles. I chuckled as I returned to the bedroom to see six eyeballs peeking from under the covers and a black tail poking out the side. Abe was completely buried out of sight with his head now under my pillow. Mom was on her smartphone checking the radar. I lit the four candles on our dresser and lay across the end of the bed. "I think that was the worst of it," Dona softly whispered. "The rest should just be rain." As uncomfortable as I was, I quickly drifted back to sleep, convinced that all was good.

I woke up with a cute little two-year-old foot stuck in my face, a sunbeam hitting me in the left eyeball, and a stiff crick in my neck. I slid off the bed, about to sneak out of the room, when I saw the covers moving in a rhythmic side-to-side pattern, and I knew that Abe was wagging his tail. "Get out here," I blurted. Abe army-crawled to the side of the bed and squirmed out from under the covers like a river otter sliding out of a pond.

"Some watch dog you are," I declared as I grabbed my clothes from the dresser. Almost immediately, Abe pounced over to the bedroom window and brushed back the curtain to look under the window shade. Instantly, his tail stopped wagging, and I knew something was amiss.

I made my way over to Abe and pulled the window shade string. To my surprise, I saw seven Holstein cows meandering down the side of our road. They were all head to tail with the boss cow in the lead, and she was in a hurried trot. I quickly pulled on my jeans and grabbed a shirt with one hand while I gently shook Dona's shoulder with the other. Her bloodshot eyes sprang open and in a startled voice stammered, "What's wrong?"

"Can you call the neighbors and tell them their cows are walking down the road?" I replied.

"The what?"

"Cows…you know the black-and-white kind… neighbors…call them please?" I asked. "Abe and I will try to head them off."

There was no time for coffee this morning. Abe sensed my excitement and was ringing the sleigh bells by the time I got to the bottom of the stairs. I grabbed a walking stick, and we headed out the back door. As I rounded the corner of the house, the cows were nowhere in sight. However, they left behind an enormous, muddy, twelve-foot-wide trail of hoofprints dug into the soft, green lawn. It was obvious that they had turned right at our gravel driveway and were headed down the field road toward the marsh.

"If they get into the marsh, we won't get them out, Abe. We better hurry," I said as my walk turned into a jog.

About halfway down the tractor path that led to the sugar bush, the trail of hoofprints disappeared into the adjoining cornfield. At that moment, I couldn't decide if that was good news or bad news. On one hand, the cornfield, filled with seven-foot-tall field corn, should slow them down so they don't reach the swamp. On the other hand, the cornfield was a good twenty acres across and the phrase "finding a needle in a haystack" instantly crossed my mind.

"Good Lord, Abe. We will never find them in there," I wheezed as I stopped running and bent over to hold my stomach and try to catch my breath. Abe continued into the corn with his nose to the ground and, a few minutes later, appeared back on the field road. He walked toward me with his tongue hanging out the side of his mouth, just as winded as I was.

"Let's head back to the house, Abe. We are going to need help on this one."

I had to leave Abe on the porch due to the mud factor, but I still got an evil eye from the wife when I walked into the kitchen with my boots on. She was sipping her coffee with her right hand and simply pointed to the door with her left. She never said a word, but I knew exactly what she meant. I felt like Abraham being kicked off of the master's bed and banished to the hallway. As I stepped off my boots on the back porch, I thought I heard Abe snicker a couple times, and he wouldn't make eye contact, so I figured that he was having a chuckle at my expense.

Walking back into the kitchen in my socks, I discovered that the neighbors were not missing any cattle. However, Dona had heard on the police scanner that a farmer named Bob over on Terrytown Road, about three miles up the hill from our farm, had reported missing cattle. The owner had followed the cow tracks to the railroad tracks and then had lost the trail when the cattle had entered the adjoining woods. Evidently, our intelligent local sheriff's department was trying to determine if it was the thunder and lightning that had spooked the animals or foul play. "They were so scared they ran right through a four-strand barbed-wire fence," Dona declared as she made her own assessment of the situation. "Sounds like they are all heifers," which in layman's terms simply means WILD, young, rebellious cows, basically teenagers. This cow-wrangling challenge just went from difficult to impossible.

After a cup of coffee, a piece of cinnamon toast, and, of course, a bowl of dog kibble on the porch, Abe and I decided to head back to the sugar bush to see if Sunflower had any news. The Mrs. had placed a call to the local sheriff's department, who in turn was going to report to Farmer Bob that we had seen the heifers come through our property. It was too wet to take the tractor because of last night's rain, so we headed out on foot, stopping briefly to bring Ada up to speed.

As we entered the woods where we tap the maple trees, we saw a very large red fox squirrel run for cover. Abe lit out after him and chased him all the way to the far end of the sugar bush. By the time I caught up with him, he had treed the squirrel and was circling the tree trunk. "Cows, Abraham, not squirrels!" I reminded him.

From behind me, I heard the gruff voice of Sunflower ask, "Cows, did ya say? Ain't yoos two out and about a bit early dis morning? What brings yoos to my neck of da woods?"

I turned around to see Sunflower digging into an old, rotted stump of a red elm tree about five feet away. I'm guessing she was looking for breakfast in the form of grubs or worms, so I asked, "What's for breakfast?"

"Voles," she fired back and went right back to digging.

"I suppose you had your fill of night crawlers last night with all this rain."

"Yup," she quipped. "Got me a full belly fur sure, by gully."

"So why are you terrorizing a poor, helpless…did you say vole?" I asked.

"Dessert!" she fired back.

"Guess I never looked at voles quite that way. By the way,

we are looking for a herd of heifers that are running around the neighborhood. You seen anything? They were headed this way."

"Just you and yoos squirrel dog. I've been in da marsh all night by gully. Ain't seen no heifer cows. Holy cryin' yoos ain't gunna shoot em, are ya?" she snapped.

"What is it with me shooting things? No, I ain't gonna shoot them. If you see anything after your dessert, just tell Ada so we can catch these critters!" I said in a frustrated tone. "I think they are in the south cornfield."

"Okey-dokey," she said with her nose full of dirt and went right back to digging.

"Come on, Abe, let's circle the cornfield." At that, Abe gave up on Mr. Squirrel and took off in a trot, staying about fifty yards ahead of me, but looking back once in a while to make sure I was following his lead.

About halfway back to the farmstead, I saw Abraham stop and turn toward the cornfield. When I caught up to him, I could hear the faint snap and crunch of cornstalks. "Sounds like our teenagers," I said. "How do you think we should go about this?"

Bending down with one knee to the ground and resting my arm on Abe's back, I thought back to a time in my youth. When I was a kid visiting Grandpa's farm years ago, he used to take me with him to check on his heifers that were pastured up on Maple Hill at the Rocky-Top Ranch. He rented property on Denzer Road that had plenty of lush, green grass and cold, spring water to "summer" his young stock. About every two weeks, he would drive his orange-colored Chevy pickup over to the summer pasture to check the fence line for breaks in the barbed wire and to make sure that the cattle still had a supply of water in the creek. He would always bring a couple sacks of ground corn feed with him.

Pulling off the road, we would park just outside an iron gate. I would climb up to the top of the gate while he climbed over to fill a wooden feed bunk with the ground corn he had brought with him. After returning the empty gunnysacks to the bed of the pickup, he would join me at the top of the gate and call for the heifers by yelling, "Come, boss, come, boss, come, boss!" His voice would carry across the valley and echo against the nearby hills. To my amazement, his voice was instantly recognized by the lead heifer, the boss cow. She would come running out of the woods. Since she was the leader of the pack, all of the other heifers would follow, running behind her. The sound of my grandpa's voice meant food to the young heifers. Standing with me at the top of the iron gate, he would count out loud the number of young cows pushing their way around the feeder. Could it be that simple with these young ladies?

"Abe, I wander if these gals will respond to a cow call?" I asked.

At that, I cupped my hands around my mouth and yelled, "Come, boss, come, boss, come, boss." Nothing happened except that we could no longer hear any cornstalks being broken. After several minutes of absolute silence, I decided to try again and called, "Come, boss, come, boss, come, boss." To my astonishment, we began to hear a lot of cornstalks being broken, and the sound was getting closer and closer.

"I think it's working, Abe."

Within two minutes, I saw a young heifer poke her head out of the corn about seventy-five yards up the road and look down the tractor path at Abe and me. I called a third time, but she did not come any closer. Thinking that maybe she was not so fond of my dog, I advised Abe to start walking toward the farm. Sure enough, as soon as Abe and I started toward the farm, she followed. Within seconds, all seven were nose to tail behind us like ducklings all in a row. The only difference was Abe was now the "boss" cow.

As we rounded the corner of the barn, a diesel-powered dually towing a rusty brown horse trailer pulled into the driveway. The runaway heifers stopped to graze on the green lawn south of the barn and gave me an opportunity to open the rear sliding barn door. Farmer Bob carried over a sack of ground feed and walked into the open door. As he did, I chuckled to myself, listening to him calling to his heifers exactly as Grandpa had taught me.

He yelled, "Come, boss, come, boss," while he shook the bag of feed out onto the concrete floor. All seven heifers followed him into the dairy barn like it was their own. After the door was closed behind them, the trailer was backed up to the barn door and all runaways were loaded without incident.

A simple handshake and a pat on Abe's head was all the reward we needed from Farmer Bob. As he drove out the driveway in a cloud of black diesel smoke, he gave us a wave of thanks out his truck window. I waved back as Abe let out his own bark of goodbye.

"Well, that was a morning to remember," I said. "Let's go get some lunch."

*There's just something wonderful about getting a small group of people together in an isolated location, and there's something about cabins themselves that imply both horror and fun.*
*– Drew Goddard*

# The River Cabin

Having loaded the car, we were headed to western Wisconsin for a few June-bug days on the Wisconsin River. This mini-vacation had been planned for months, and it included a three-day float trip with two nights of sandbar camping and an extended stay at the river cabin.

A few years ago, this part of the country was affected by a recession. The property value in the housing market was hit especially hard. While detrimental to many, two positive results for our family were that people offered to sell property at a very reasonable price and that interest rates plummeted to an all-time low. This happened to come at a time when our family had been looking for property along the Wisconsin River in southwestern Wisconsin, property for relaxation and recreation. This was our frugal way of investing in vacation property, property that was not too far away and offered us a unique way to relax for river corridor activities.

I spent most of my childhood growing up in the Sauk-

Prairie area northwest of Madison along the Wisconsin River. During this time, I grew to love not only the river itself, but the nature that surrounded the river. It probably started with our family outings swimming behind the bowling alley. As a kid, and with little respect for the strong undercurrent of the river just below the Prairie du Sac Dam, I would push the limits of how far my parents would let me wade out into deeper water on the river.

Over the years, the river has embedded many memories on my brain, such as the day my grandfather took me fishing below the railroad bridge in Sauk City. This section of the river was a forbidden place to us as kids. According to our mother, there were swirling river currents caused by the wide river being constricted through the narrow passages under the bridge. It was the wrong place for any "tomfoolery." Don't tell Mom, but the excitement of doing something forbidden with her own father was very exhilarating to the son. I believe it was the first time I ever used artificial lures to catch fish. Thanks, Gramps!

Probably the greatest influence of the river in my youth came from canoe trips down the great Wisconsin. They were called "float trips" by the adults, but to a teenager, floating was a boring way to use a canoe. Canoes were made for adventure, not floating. If the trip was deemed a six-mile float trip, my canoe was paddled over twice that distance. I didn't just go downstream on the river, I went sideways and upstream and into all the tributaries and around stumps and through downed trees. The trick was getting a canoe partner that was as adventuresome and talented as I was.

On float trips over the years, I've had a water snake fall off a tree into a canoe, been swarmed by paper wasps after bumping into their nest, and once touched a sleeping whitetail fawn in the long grass on the riverbank. I've seen bald eagles catch fish and pass them midair to their mates, I've been dive-bombed by great blue herons as they relieved themselves in a flyover, I've heard the chilling sound of the great horned owl at night, and I've seen millions of bats fly in a midsummer mating frenzy over the water. I've seen skinny dippers that weren't so skinny and watched fireworks over the water on the Fourth of July from a canoe.

The focus of our family's search for property was on a special part of the river called the Lower Wisconsin State Riverway, between Sauk Prairie and Wyalusing State Park as it flows into the mighty Mississippi just south of Prairie du Chien. While the Wisconsin River is known as the hardest-working river in Wisconsin because of the hydroelectric dams, this 92-mile section of the river is unimpeded all the way to the Mississippi River. It is also a part of the river that has special regulations governing what can and cannot be done or built along the riverbanks. This attracted our family because we knew this protection of nature would attract more wildlife and offer thousands of acres of State Nature Area to explore.

Our property search eventually paid off with the purchase of four acres in a small development called Almar Acres, located between Gotham and Orion. This wooded property came with a modest cedar cabin and a huge sandstone-dolomite fireplace. Over the first years, we acquired several free or inexpensive boats to take to the cabin. Currently, we store two canoes, two kayaks, and a flat-bottom boat there. As every vacation property deserves a title, we appropriately named it *The River Cabin*. We have established our "Escape to Wisconsin" getaway and have furnished it with the river vehicles we need to enjoy it.

Abraham loved to travel in a vehicle. Travel meant smelling new things, meeting different people, and often eating new and different foods, although he never seemed to eat his kibble at the cabin. His excitement started as soon as I grabbed my duffel bag to begin packing. The first thing he did was guard the back door. Once he was outside and the car door was opened to load the luggage, he climbed into the front seat. It made no difference to him that we may not leave for three more hours; he would not vacate the front seat of the car. He was diligent in making sure that we did not leave without him. He did seem to grumble, however, when the Mrs. made him move to the back seat.

Lots of things were going with us today. Not only were we spending time on the river, but, as I mentioned already, we were planning an extended stay at our cabin. Plans were for seventeen days. Seventeen days of food and beverages, fishing gear, camping gear, sunscreen, swimming gear, not to mention all the canoe gear we would pick up at the cabin. Abe's back-seat space had diminished ever so quickly in the last hour, and he was looking concerned. With a pat on the head, I assured him that there was plenty of space for him to nap between the boxes of groceries on the two-hour drive.

A long five hours later, while we were not on schedule, we were finally on our way. Ten o'clock in the morning was the plan, but one in the afternoon would work just as well. As we headed down the driveway, I noticed that Ada was watching from her favorite log behind the barn. This was the first time we would be gone from the farm since we met her four months ago. I pondered for a moment what she might be thinking in a few days when we weren't around to talk with her. I quickly surmised that she had already lived on our farm for two years of her life before Abe and I met her. She probably knew exactly what to expect and was looking forward to some genuine, good old-fashioned woodchuck time. We would certainly miss her company, but I was confident she would fill us in on all the details upon our return to the farm.

*But now ask the beasts, and let them teach you;*
*And the birds of the heavens and let them tell you.*
*– Job 12:7*

# Squirrels on the Roof

As soon as we pulled off the highway and onto the river road, Abe sat up and stretched. His tail began to thump with excitement against the cardboard box of groceries next to him. For most of the trip, he stayed curled up in a tight ball with his nose tucked under his tail, at times snoring louder than the music on the car radio. It wasn't the change in blacktop under the tires, but that large, black nose that told him we were close to our cabin. My guess was that the thriving squirrel population alerted him, which was the same reason that made the cabin so much fun for him. Hours were spent each day at the cabin making sure the squirrels stayed up a tree or off his property.

At the mere sight of the cabin, I felt my body relax. Sure, we had a lot of work ahead of us to get the canoe loaded and to check on the mouse and bat population, but the cabin brought a slower pace. Our cabin was a simple, large, one-room building. The front door opened into the kitchen area under the loft. This took up half of the cabin's square footage, while the back half of the cabin was a living room accented with a fantastic fieldstone fireplace. Leading up to the loft on the west wall was a staircase that turned in front of the west window. If Abraham was in the cabin, that was exactly where you would find him. From the vantage point of the stairs, he could see out two windows at once, not only the one on the west side but also the one on the east side of the cabin. He would usually lay on the stair landing for hours, drifting in and out of sleep, watching and waiting.

Several times a day, Abe would suddenly spring to life. He started to whine, quiver, and look at me with raised ears and wide-open eyes. Not from his words, but by his excitement, I could hear him tell me, "Master, there is a squirrel on the roof!"

This was the most exciting time at the cabin for Abe. He had taken it upon himself; it was his responsibility to ensure that those tree rats never made it off his property alive. Maybe that was his way of protecting the family, maybe it was just a big game, but by the time I made it to the front door to let him out, he was usually going berserk. My guess was that the squirrels egged him on through the window. He literally began jumping up and down with anticipation, telling me with his body language to "hurry up!"

At the touch of the doorknob, Abe's entire body language transformed from playful puppy to dead serious killer. His ears suddenly laid back, the hair on his back stood straight up, and he crouched down in an attack posture. I usually teased him by saying, "Don't let him get away...are you ready?" The door flew open, and he bounded from the cabin. I heard his claws grinding on the concrete stoop and all four feet digging as fast as they could go. Up on the cedar shake roof, I immediately heard the squirrel take off, scrambling for the oak tree at the north end of the cabin.

In order for a squirrel to get off the cabin roof, there was a ten-foot "leap of faith" necessary to reach the nearest tree. The obvious safe way to exit the roof was to jump down to the lower flat roof over the utility room and onto the canoe that was mounted to the north cabin wall. From the aluminum canoe, it was a short four-foot drop to the soft, sandy soil. Was it worth the risk to go for the oak, or was the bushy-tail fast enough to reach the canoe before Abe rounded the corner? This was the chase game we played three times each day at the cabin.

After several years of this peculiar entertainment, I started wondering if there was more to this ritual. Why in the first place would the silly squirrel climb onto the cabin roof? It wasn't easy to get on the roof from an overhanging branch off the blue spruce out front. There were no acorns or seed pods for food up there. It was not a shortcut to anywhere. I often saw two or more of these gray squirrels high up in majestic white oaks on the edge of our property line chattering and flicking their tails almost any time of day. From the ground level, I couldn't hear anything but a few long cries and some short barks, but my guess was the conversation went something like this: "Hey, you want to mess with that dog again? Bet you can't sneak across the cabin roof without him hearing you."

You could almost set your watch to the times of day this game took place, usually early after sunrise, again at lunchtime, and one more attempt about an hour before sunset. Why was it played so systematically? Was there a reason why they toyed with Abe three times a day? And another thing, why was it that no squirrel ever perished? Never! No matter how many missed the oak tree and belly flopped to the ground or were pummeled as dog and squirrel crossed paths beneath the canoe, they all seemed to survive the ordeal. Yes, maybe they were a little bruised, but they all made it to the safety of the oak savanna at the top of the hill to play another day.

Today, I was determined to get on top of the situation. So instead of watching the game from the kitchen window like I usually did, I quickly ran around the east side of the cabin while Abe headed around the west side doing his growling and huffing. Fifty-year-old legs don't move as quickly as four-year-old dog legs, but I impressed myself when I made it around the back corner just in time to see a beautiful gray squirrel flying through the air. He had made the leap of faith toward the lone oak. His front feet were fully extended forward, ears laid back, and his charcoal-gray tail was as straight as an arrow, making his body an aerodynamic, fluffy spear. I saw his outstretched front paws ready to grab tree bark. Don't tell Abe, but I have to admit that I was rooting for the squirrel to make a safe landing on the oak tree.

He had made a beautiful leap from the peak of the roof twenty feet up. The elegance of a confident squirrel flying through the air was something spectacular to see! But that all changed when said squirrel realized his landing was going to be anything but glamorous. All of a sudden, the sleek, aerodynamic tree rat, who a second ago was confident of his landing, was now flailing in the wind for any piece of real estate that might save him from Canine Terra Firma directly beneath him. The mighty black dog was positioned and ready, teeth showing and growling. This was not going to end well!

Mr. Gray hit the ground with a thud. I grabbed my stomach as I contemplated his pain. I fully expected that the squirrel was about to be shook like a rag doll, but I was stopped dead in my tracks when I thought I heard Abe say one little word... "Loser." The winded squirrel slowly crawled away and gingerly creeped up the oak tree. Almost immediately, I was hit on the head with something. Something was raining down from above. Abe quickly gobbled up what had fallen to the ground, and as the last morsel disappeared, I realized what it was and how this game was played. Sitting near the top of the oak were three gray squirrels. They were the referees to this spectacle and had dropped the reward that Abe had earned...three squirrel mouths full of cat food.

The game was played, not to vindicate the property of any vermin who violated the cabin rooftop, but to win the race to the oak tree. Winner takes all! Squirrel wins, squirrel eats. Abe wins, Abe eats, not squirrel but the cat food stolen from Sophia's house by the boat landing. Cat food was the physical reward, but pride was the ultimate reward.

Both squirrel and dog hated the tabby that terrorized the wildlife along the river. He was the "pride and joy" of Sophia, a retired doctor who lived in a mansion overlooking the Wisconsin River. Sophia was a great neighbor and always took time to scratch Abe behind the ears or pat him on the back, but that cat was a nightmare. The tabby, one whose name we shall not speak of, not only killed but tortured any creature that was unfortunate to cross its path. The first and only time that Abe paid his respect to Sophia's tabby, he was rewarded with a bloody swipe to the old black nose that drew a loud "Yipe!" and a quick retreat.

This spoiled tabby was generously and religiously fed

gourmet food three times a day on the back deck above the boat dock. Unfortunately for the tabby, the squirrels in Almar Acres would do anything and everything to antagonize him. So, they started stealing his food. Wanting to get Abe in on the take, they needed a way to get him out of the house to share the plunder. I soon realized that I was the one who was being played. I'll admit it, dog and squirrel working together had me in the palms of their hands…or was it the soft pads of their feet?

Anyway, it was a simple, fun game of tag, and today Abe had won. "Loser!" brought a plethora of kibble from Abe's furry-tailed friends up to three times a day. No wonder he never ate his dog food at the cabin.

*At the beach, life is different. Time doesn't move hour by hour but mood to moment. We live by the currents, plan by the tides, and follow the sun.*
*– Sandy Gingras*

# Sandbars

If conditions were right and the opportunity presented itself, you would find us out on the Wisconsin River on many a summer day. If we could have it our way, we would get away every weekend, but life was just plain busy. Getting away was almost always a struggle and often took strategic planning. In addition to finding spare time, the river itself and the ever-changing weather conditions would also have to cooperate.

The last 92-mile stretch of the Lower Wisconsin State Riverway was the only section of the river that was unobstructed by man-made dams. Therefore, the river level downstream from the last dam fluctuated on a daily basis. Local rain was usually no problem, but upstream rain could be a big problem. If there was excessive rain in northern or central Wisconsin, the upstream dams would be opened to allow excess tributary water to pass downstream. Knowledge of the river level was critical when planning an event on the Lower Wisconsin.

The attraction of the river to our family was the sandbars. If the river level was too high, sandbars did not exist. Fortunately for us, there was a United States Geological Survey (USGS) river gage two miles downstream from our cabin. To organize a river excursion, we needed three things: time off work, the river gage reading, and a favorable upstream weather report. My interpretation of a fun weekend river excursion required a three-day weekend with no rain in the forecast and a Muscoda gage reading of 7,000 cfs (cubic feet per second) or less. And that was exactly what we were looking forward to...a three-day canoe and two-night camping trip!

Why are the sandbars so popular, you ask? They are absolutely the only way to have an entire island to yourself for picnicking, fishing, and overnight camping. The Lower Wisconsin is a unique, protected area with thousands of acres designated as a State Natural Area. It is a great way to get away from the hassle of everyday life and spend some time in the great outdoors. Sometimes we would invite family or friends to go with us for a few days on the river. We get a kick out of watching city folks deal with untamed, raw nature. However, for this particular weekend, it would just be the Mr., the Mrs., and the dog.

Abe had been sitting in the driver's seat guarding his shuttle reservation for the last hour and was excited to move to the back seat. For this float trip, we planned to paddle twenty-seven miles of river, ending at the cabin boat landing in Almar Acres. The weather forecast looked great, and the company couldn't have been better. Abe agreed! The seventeen-foot canoe we called *Rodie* was quickly loaded on the roof of the car, and life jackets, paddles, a cooler of food and beverages, a tent, sleeping bags, and other glamping essentials were added to the trunk.

After two quick stops, one for fresh sweet corn and one for adult beverages, we portaged upstream and arrived at our launching point by 10am. As Dona and I unloaded the canoe from the car top, Abe went off exploring. We systematically went over a prepared checklist to make sure we had all the essentials that make life comfortable on the river and quickly loaded them into the canoe. The level of excitement and anticipation was high. I reminded Abe that he wouldn't see dry land for several hours and how the water could affect him, if you know what I mean. After he visited the nearest tree, he gingerly climbed into the rear of the canoe and groaned at the lack of space he was allowed. Several minutes of *rock the boat* finally gained our canoeing confidence, and we quickly caught up with the current on the river.

As I stated earlier, this was more like a float trip than a youthful canoe trip. Sure, the goal was to reach the cabin downstream, but we were in no hurry to get there. Within minutes of our launch, the wife had her paddle across her lap and her feet up on the bow of the canoe. The only job for the boys in the rear of the canoe was to avoid obstacles along the riverbank. The midmorning sun felt warm, and there was a slight breeze blowing across the river. Abe rested his head on my lap and soon drifted off to sleep.

I can handle a lot of uncomfortable situations on a canoe/camping trip, such as bugs or a lost piece of essential equipment, but one thing that can quickly ruin my fun is a sunburn. You might think that I would be floating down the Wisconsin in a speedo, trying to soak up as much sun as possible, but not this camper. Today, we expected slightly overcast skies, but mostly full sun. That required a sun hat, long-sleeve cotton shirt, beach towel over the legs, and polarized sunglasses on a tether. The Mrs. was sporting her American flag bikini for a bit of sun this morning after being slathered in sunscreen lotion, but was prepared for the midday cover-up to ward off a burn.

We have never kept an accurate count, but this was probably our 12th or 13th trip on this stretch of the river, so confidence was high. The river level was an ideal 6,700 cfs, and sandbars were plentiful. By noon, we had already beached up to one for lunch. Abe quickly jumped out of the boat and found a few minnows to torment. He thought that pouncing on them was the appropriate response, but only caught a beak full of water for his efforts. Barking at them didn't seem to help either. He convinced me that it was time to get wet, so while Dona spread a blanket on the sand for lunch, we hit the warm shallows for a quick swim and a short game of water fetch.

A few minutes later, just as I was about to toss the stick one more time, I suddenly saw Abe look over to Dona, and I knew that she had called us for lunch. "Lunch is ready" brought us quickly back to the blanket only to be denied access. It seemed that wet and sandy dog on the beach had about the same favor as wet and muddy dog in the house. That was ok, Abe and I loved having our lunch catered to us. We chose real estate on the river's edge so our feet could rest in the current of the river. Abe sat right beside me, and we leaned against each other for stability in the shifting sand. Our menu today was sand-sandwiches, sharp cheddar cheese, seedless grapes, and a glass of Pinot Grigio in a plastic cup (no glass allowed on the river). Our lunch was generously delivered to us at water's edge by one voluptuous flag lady, which we proudly saluted. After a relaxing meal and a quick nap in the sun to dry out the swim shorts, more sunscreen was applied and we were again headed down the magnificent Wisconsin.

*The farther one gets into the wilderness, the greater is the attraction*
*of its lonely freedom. – Theodore Roosevelt*

# Camping

If you like the outdoors, if you like rustic camping, if you like exploring, if you like privacy, if you like adventure, then you will love sandbar camping. This is not something you can do on most rivers and is somewhat unique to the southern part of the Wisconsin River. Even at that, it is not something that can be done all spring, summer, or fall due to river levels. There are times of the year when the river seems to be void of kayaks and canoes, flat-bottom boats and pontoons. There are times when the river seems to be infested with the same. The trick is learning when, where, and how to find your own fun and privacy.

While our family owns a 15-foot flat-bottom fishing boat with a Beavertail motor for fishing on the river, it is the use of kayaks and canoes that we prefer on the mighty Wisconsin. The silent movement through the water permits more wildlife viewing and seems to soothe the soul from the business of life. Although, using a canoe to haul your camping gear to your campsite has its challenges. How much should you take? Can you keep everything dry? Will you be comfortable? What happens if the weather gets nasty? Questions you may not be able to answer until you simply try it yourself. The same is true for us. In fact, even though Abe and I consider ourselves seasoned campers, we admit that we learn something new each time we venture out on the river.

If there was one thing we learned early on the river, it was "first come, first served!" You do not want to canoe until dusk and then hope to find a private sandbar that fits all your camping requirements, especially if you have a group of people or a playful puppy in your party. Our practice was to start early, stop early. Today we began looking for our camping sandbar by 2pm. We have calculated our two nights of camping to fall within two narrow parts of the river, ten miles apart, and by early afternoon we were safely inside that travel window.

If you compared notes among people that sandbar camp on the Wisconsin River, you would quickly learn that not everyone agrees on the same set of parameters. Our family searches for locations with little traffic or road noise, no houses within sight, shallow beach on the upstream end, a sharp drop-off on the downstream end, and no parallel sandbars. Wind can be another issue. Sometimes it's good to camp on a moist sandbar instead of one that has loose sand that can blast the skin off your body and imbed itself in every piece of food you brought with you. I'll admit that sand adds a unique crunch to the sandwich, but it is not welcome in mine or Abe's.

We also avoid spots with a parallel sandbar or sandy beach shoreline. With just the three of us camping, we don't care to have other people within sight of our location. This allows for a more relaxing and, need I say, exotic camping. The shallow beach upstream is for bathing and swimming, and the drop-off downstream is for catching a few smallies or catfish. Sometimes we get all of the above, and sometimes we don't. On a few occasions, we thought that we picked the perfect location only to have a group of rivergoers join our sandbar late in the day, stealing our privacy. Then again, on another trip, we got started late in the day and had to pick a sandbar after dark. We had no idea if it was a good spot, and it ended up being one of our more memorable trips.

It's probably worth mentioning how the outdoor restroom works on the river. One technique is to find a vegetated area for privacy. Another is to carry a portable latrine, which is desired by the ladies more than the men for obvious reasons. While canoeing, we gauge our bathroom stops with how much traffic is on the river. It's not a lot of fun to wave to sightseers looking through binoculars while you're squatting in the bush. If trees are available, we have simply tied up a tarp that provides limited, but adequate, privacy. A good rule of thumb is to carry in, carry out, and bury waste…dog waste also! We leave sandbars like we want to find them, free of garbage and waste. We often carry out other people's garbage to clean up for the next travelers. It's not a burden, it's a privilege!

When camping on a sandbar, we are almost always blessed with spectacular sounds in nature. We often hear the chilling cry of coyotes and the soothing call of barred owls during the night. We like to sleep to the sound of water flowing over a nearby log and the crackling of the campfire outside the tent. By pitching our tent away from vegetation, we can leave the tent door open without the risk of mosquitoes or flies as we listen to a chorus of frogs and crickets. Sunrise brings the sounds of sandhill cranes, Canadian geese, and bald eagles. Sometimes it is just better to keep quiet and let nature do the talking. But, don't forget to keep your eyes open for the silent box turtles, water snakes, and daddy longlegs that may stop for a visit. Most everything is harmless and just as curious about us as we are about them.

After a six-hour float trip today, we had reached our target location for sandbar camping and picked a sandbar that fit all desired criterion. Having no luck with the fishing pole in the early afternoon, I turned my attention to collecting some wood for the campfire. The first night out is our big meal of the trip, usually something special. Tonight, it would be grilled shrimp and corn on the cob. As it got dark, we could see a full sky of stars, but the moon wouldn't show up until the wee early morning. It was getting very dark very fast. Before the corn was thoroughly cooked, it was completely dark. We could see the faint glow of two other campfires in the far distance, but no one was close to us. We had the perfect setup tonight. No road noise, no bugs, a large sandbar, and lots of privacy.

Well, just when we thought we had everything under control, the unexpected happened. The corn and shrimp were cooking nicely on the fire, the stars were out against clear skies, warm evening with no bugs, barred owls calling in the distance, nice fire with plenty of spare wood, wine was flowing, good buzz on, and spirits were high. We had purposely purchased large skin-on shrimp to grill over the open wood fire. What we did not expect was such a dark night. So there we sat, actually kneeling in the sand, buck naked, tipsy on wine in the pitch dark night, and the shrimp wouldn't peel! No matter what we tried, we could not get the shell off the shrimp. Giggling with frustration and salivating at the buttery smell, we couldn't eat our rock shrimp. We even tried chewing them whole and spitting out the shell to no avail. I guess it's just corn on the cob for supper tonight.

Another successful sandbar camping adventure!

*Look deep into nature, and then you will*
*understand everything better.*
*– Albert Einstein*

# Call of the Wild

As usual, Abe had me awake at 6:17am. Hoping to sleep another hour, and since the tent door was wide open all night, I tried to convince him that there was no need for me to take him outside. He was welcome to go for a walk all by himself, but he declined. He groaned in disappointment and settled back down on the end of my sleeping bag.

The river was incredible this morning! There was a thick, misty fog floating over the entire river valley. The campfire was still smoking from last night's failed shrimp boil. The sound of sandhill cranes filled the air in a low flyover, returning a few moments later and landing at the far end of our island sandbar. Abe wanted to leave the tent and give chase, but I convinced him to just lie still and listen.

A few minutes later, after incessant whining from man's best friend, I stepped out for the morning call of the wild. The two of us snuck out of the tent silently so the Mrs. could continue her slumber. Due to the thickness of the fog this morning, there was no hurry to get dressed. I couldn't see thirty feet in front of me, so there wouldn't be anyone out on the river this early. It was simply too dangerous.

I had all the intentions of joining Abe in a morning swim until my toes discovered that the river water was much cooler than my sleeping bag. I was lost in thought, enjoying the sounds of the morning and the relief of nature at the water's edge, when I heard a female voice come from my left say, "Good morning." Startled to the point of mid-stream interruption, unable to move, I muttered something unintelligible to a young couple that passed by me in a canoe not five feet in front of my carcass in all its glory. Abe let out a quiet bark with tail in full wag. I think he was hoping they would stop and have breakfast, but they faded off into the misty fog as quickly as they had appeared.

"Thanks a lot," I stammered as I looked down at my dog still wagging his tail and staring downstream. "You could've warned me!" Nothing, not even a concerned look, came from that dog, although I'm pretty sure he was laughing. Immediately, the sandhills let out their own cry of laughter and took a running start for the skies. I reached in the tent, grabbed my sweats just to be safe, and began stoking the fire. By the time the coffeepot began to perk, I was laughing too. After swearing Abe to secrecy, the two of us settled down for some very black coffee. Listening to the sounds of the river, sipping on my second cup of coffee, I patted Abe on the head and said, "It just doesn't get better than this, does it, old boy?" A few seconds later, a sexy voice from the tent said, "Come back to bed, cowboy."

Winking at Abraham, I blurted, "I stand corrected!"

*When you're young, thunderstorms seem scary. Like the sky is angry*
*at you. But now that I'm older, something about its roar soothes me; it's*
*comforting to know that even nature needs to scream sometimes.*
*– Author Unknown ("This is the Life I Have Chosen")*

# Mystery Thunderstorm

Indeed, the morning had a slow start. I knew from such a heavy fog that everything would be wet. That meant that we had to dry things off before packing them back into the canoe. No one seemed to be all that anxious to get back on the river. I slowly rolled up the sleeping bags and put them inside their waterproof bags. The tent was collapsed, dried, and stored at the bottom of the canoe. The cooking utensils were organized and packed away along with the food, clothing, and fishing gear.

I don't remember what time we actually launched from our perfect sandbar campsite, but I did notice that many a canoe passed us by. "It might be a bit more difficult to find a sandbar this afternoon with all this river traffic," I said as I laid my paddle across the thwart and climbed into the back seat. To our advantage, we usually traveled less distance on the river than most people. They actually paddled their canoes while we more or less floated at the mercy of the river current. To make myself feel better, I determined that they would have passed us during the day anyway. We intended about ten miles, and they most likely would be going fifteen miles or more. I wondered why in the world they were in such a hurry this morning. Oh well, more river for just the three of us.

Since it was only an hour or two before lunchtime, we decided to snack on the boat and only stop when we needed to stretch our legs. Abe was all about the snacks. Usually, the food was located near the front passenger and the beverages near the rear passengers, but today it was just the opposite. The food was back with the boys. Each time I dug into the food cooler, there was a black, wet nose in there helping me. To get a snack to the Mrs., we would place it on a canoe paddle and carefully slide it forward to the front. Drinks came back to us the same way or were just floated alongside the boat. Dona had packed a plethora of snacks. We had chips, candy bars, energy bars, nuts, fruit, cheese, veggies, and Abe's favorite, beef jerky. The beverages included water, wine, orange juice, milk, and a variety of diet soda. The trick on a three-day trip was to always save some snacks to be brand new each day. Today it was smoked string cheese and peppered beef jerky. Abe was elated!

We had brought a smartphone with us, but left it turned off and packed away. We used it on the river for two purposes, to take pictures and to confirm our location with the GPS. Sometimes a passerby needed assistance getting to a certain place at a certain time. We have entertained questions like, "How far is it to the next boat landing?" or "Where is the nearest bathroom?" Since most of the morning's river traffic was ahead of us and most of our pictures had been taken yesterday, we had no need for the phone. It was best left conserving battery life, tucked away in a waterproof thwart bag.

About two o'clock in the afternoon, the wind started blowing upstream. It gradually became more aggressive so that there were whitecaps on a few waves mid-river. We started hugging the shoreline and actually had to paddle the canoe to make forward progress. Pretty soon, we were struggling to keep the boat pointed forward.

"Let's make for that sandbar ahead," I yelled. "We might as well wait out this wind."

It was more of a struggle than I expected to reach the sandbar, but we made it across a full river of whitecaps that flirted with reaching the gunnels. On normal summer days, there were occasional gusts on the river, but something about this wind was unusual. Having made shore, the wife immediately dug for the phone. By the time she had it booted up, we heard thunder from the south.

"We're in trouble," she declared. "A major storm cell is almost on top of us."

Now what should we do? We found ourselves in a precarious situation, stranded in the middle of a river on a barren island of sand with a dog who hates thunder and an aluminum canoe.

"Let's get out of this lightning rod," I proclaimed. We quickly dragged the canoe as far onto shore as we could and grabbed the portable latrine. "Leave everything in the canoe," I said. "Maybe the extra weight will keep it from blowing away."

Now, a word of explanation is in order. To seek our safety on a barren sandbar void of trees and vegetation, we had grabbed the portable latrine. This consisted of a self-expanding three-foot by three-foot dressing room about seven feet tall. It was made from the same material as a nylon tent with an open floor and a zippered door. It was designed to be used as a dressing room on the beach or as a latrine on a sandbar. It fit one person comfortably, but two adults and a scared black dog not so comfortably. While it protected fairly well from the bite of blowing sand, it was not a storm shelter!

By now, we could hear tempestuous straight-line winds coming through the trees, getting closer and closer with each second. It sounded like King Kong was about to step out of the tree line. Large, tall trees were nearly bent to the point of breaking, and it was raining sideways. The thunder was continuous, and lightning seemed to streak across the entire skyline. Both of us were hanging onto the flimsy nylon latrine to keep it upright, expecting to be picked up off the ground at any second in a whirlwind. Abe was shivering uncontrollably and whimpering. It was raining so hard I could no longer see the canoe fifty feet away and we were soaked to the bone, even inside the shelter. It took a long twenty minutes for the storm to pass and the rain and wind to finally subside.

As the storm moved upstream, Dona checked her now-soaked phone for radar, but there was no reception and no data available. We had no idea if more was yet to come or if the beast had passed. We had a decision to make, and it had to be made quickly. We decided to fold the latrine, bail the water from the canoe, and head for the north shore. Fortunately, we knew exactly where we were on the river. A boat landing and civilization were less than two miles downstream. Whether right or wrong, we decided in an instant that we were too vulnerable to stay out in the open. "Let's go for the boat landing," I nervously mumbled. Abe was the first one in the canoe!

I'm not sure if we have ever paddled as hard as we did that day. The waves were still rough, and the wind was still blowing upstream against us. We were about halfway to shore when we spotted another canoe of victims floundering in the wind. I waved my arms to get their attention and yelled across the water that there was a boat landing directly ahead. We all agreed that we should get there as quickly as possible and that hugging the north shore would prepare us for a quick landing if needed.

We did not make it to our refuge before another round of wind and rain had hit us, but at least the lightning remained at bay. At the boat landing, exhausted and water-logged, we met others in the same condition and quickly made friends with one who had a car. Due to the generosity of our new friends, everyone was carpooled to his own vehicle downstream. Some equipment had been lost and some egos had been softened, but everyone had survived the mystery thunderstorm that had been missed by the three-day forecast. Maybe that's why those city slickers were in such a hurry this morning?! Chalk up another eventful and memorable adventure on the Lower Wisconsin State Riverway.

*If we walk in the woods, we*
*must feed mosquitoes. – Ralph Waldo Emerson*

# God Bless Mosquitoes

Why did God create mosquitoes? While they may be a link in the chain of life for little brown bats, bluegills, purple martins, and smallmouth bass, I have to think that most creatures will continue to thrive without the mighty mosquito on their menu. As an avid outdoorsman, I can handle most blood-sucking creatures found in Wisconsin such as freshwater leeches, wood ticks, and horseflies. The mosquito, however, is in a class of its own. "Hated" by most is probably an understatement! Maybe it's because there are so many of them, or maybe it's because they seem to hunt the human body and hit you when and where you are the most vulnerable. They quickly find any exposed skin, whether it's at the top of the sock line or smack dab in the center of your forehead.

And what's the itch all about? Why do we have to suffer for an extra three days after the proboscis is extracted? Isn't the bite bad enough? I bet there isn't a single place on my body that has not been violated over the last fifty-plus years.

The eyelid, the buttocks, in between fingers, and the bottom of my foot have been the most surprising. Some bites are painful, and some are just plain irritating. But why, oh why, did God create mosquitoes?

After years of pondering this question, I have concluded that it's because God has a sense of humor. Next time you slap your own forehead to kill a mosquito and come up empty, remember that God just had a good laugh. What's funnier than watching someone slap themselves? That's also why God created ice. Try not to laugh when you watch people falling on ice. It's impossible! Sure, you might outwardly act all concerned and ask, "Are you ok?" But inwardly you will be laughing.

Mosquitoes might also be God's messengers. While most of us think they are the messengers from hell, maybe we are thinking the wrong way. They say "hindsight is 20/20," meaning that it's much easier to look back in time to understand or see clearly the here and now. Permit me to explain what I mean.

While trout fishing in the Kickapoo Valley one day with some friends, we were walking through some heavy brush and got hounded by mosquitoes. They were everywhere, in the ears, mouth, and eyes, on the back of my neck, and pegging the small of my back just out of reach. I was so irritated that I took the time to stop and cover up with long pants, a collared shirt, and a head net while the rest of my friends laughed at my lack of "love of nature" as they put it. These three other friends were "man enough" to tolerate the torture, although I had a good laugh at all their swatting the rest of the day. The next day, my "love of nature" friends were not suffering from itchy bites as much as they were suffering from poison ivy. I think the Good Lord was deliberately sending us a message by way of "mosquitogram" the previous day. My point is this, maybe we should listen more attentively to things around us even though such things as the sound of a mosquito drives us up the wall.

Still not convinced? Another one of my personal hypotheses is that mosquitoes were created to test your hearing, not to drive you up a wall. The human was designed to be able to hear things down in the 30 hertz range and up to the 19,000 hertz range. However, as we get older, we tend to lose some of that range, particularly the top end. Anyone over eighty years old will confirm this gem.

Here is a test. If you want to freak out a group of kids sometime, play a ringtone on your smartphone that is 12,000 hertz or higher. If you are over fifty years old, it won't bother you at all, but the younger crowd will hold their ears in pain. It's all about the frequency. God uses the mosquito to help you hang onto your zest for life. The next time that you are annoyed by a mosquito buzzing at 600 beats per minute while you are trying to sleep, be thankful that you can still hear it. As soon as you can no longer hear a mosquito you are, well, almost dead…just saying…

God bless mosquitoes!

*If...and if...you cannot identify the next ten birds you see...*
*then, you are not living! – Andree Dubreuil*

# A Sexy Redhead

Having returned to The River Cabin a little earlier than expected, a little wet and tired but a whole lot relieved and thankful, I decided to get started on a few cabin honey-dos that had been put off since last fall. Today it would be the back utility room soffit. Cabin life is wonderful, don't get me wrong, but sometimes I second-guess the fact that we spend about as much time fixing cabin life as we do enjoying cabin life.

Soon after our cabin purchase, we started meeting other cabin neighbors. Cabin neighbors are some of the friendliest neighbors you can have. Well, most of them are. Yes, there are some who flood the borders of their properties with *No Trespassing* signs and are not welcome to any sort of visit on their doorsteps no matter how well it is intended. Yet, while a few of our cabin neighbors are shy to the general public, most are friendly to us. Some neighbors we met while canoeing on the river, some we met while out for a morning stroll, and yes, some we met during a freak thunderstorm.

Most, however, were met by taking the time and being so bold as to knock on their door.

Knocking on a stranger's door can be risky and intimidating. Will this intrusion be met with the friendly visit that was intended, or will this outreach be interpreted as a "What the hell do you want?" mentality?

Neighbor visits are like sandbar camping. What we learned on one visit was not always helpful for the next. Some people are talkers, and some are listeners. Some people are overly suspicious, and some are open and welcome. Some people come outside to meet you, and some people invite you inside to talk to them. On a few occasions, I found myself hoping that there wouldn't be anyone home to save the uneasiness or embarrassment of an awkward conversation, only to be invited in and given an impromptu tour of their entire house and shown pictures of their extended family. One lady took our boldness to meet her as her invitation to ask us to help her with things around her cabin. She was so happy to meet someone new that I ended up fixing her ceiling fan at the peak of her vaulted ceiling. She had no qualms about putting my life in jeopardy right there on the spot! But, all in all, cabin neighbors get along well with other cabin neighbors. When you own a cabin, you are automatically inducted into a unique and special club.

On one such visit, I met a good old German-American named Klaus. He took to me like a father to a son; he was probably thirty years my senior. Klaus gave me advice on cabin life whether I wanted it or not. Our visits were simply me listening to him ramble on about anything and everything. It wasn't so much that he needed to be heard, but rather that he had such a plethora of knowledge invaluable to us as new cabin owners. He didn't seem to think I had much to offer him, but he certainly had lots of advice to offer me. He was the one neighbor that informed me that, over the years, I would be spending a lot of time fixing our new-to-us cabin. He even advised me to start collecting tools at the cabin, starting immediately.

"If you need it at home, you will need it at your cabin," he declared. This man was prophetic! "Chain saw, screwdrivers, woodworking tools, plumbing tools, ladders, shovels, and much more will be needed at your cabin, even before you don't have them."

He informed me that borrowing from a neighbor was an option, but friends didn't stay friends very long if you were only at their doorstep to ask for this or that. Klaus gently gave me said advice, at the same time delivering a subliminal message that he did not want to be a lender of his precious tools. Point taken, Klaus, and thanks for all the advice!

And so it is at our cabin...a gradual collection of necessary tools to fix cabin life. This morning, as I lay in my comfy, warm log bed, my attention was curiously drawn toward the utility room soffit near the back of the cabin. I did not come to this particular fix of cabin life on my own. No, I had the help of one very sexy redhead. Not the foxy sixty-year-old at the end of our gravel road who liked to tease the boaters with her sunbathing episodes. Rather, a pesky yellow-bellied sapsucker woodpecker.

I call her pesky because she had recently been showing up every morning soon after sunrise to fill the peaceful cabin air with an alarm of thundering jackhammer percussion. She was almost as faithful as Abe and his 6:17am blow to the chest each morning. This morning, frustrated that my dreams were again rudely interrupted, I was determined to investigate what it was that attracted this redhead to the soffit at the back of the cabin.

"Coffee," I declared as I threw back the covers.

Abe replied to my statement with a loud yawn and a stretch as he lifted off his dog pillow. After I had donned a few clothes and Abe had shaken out the morning cobwebs from his black-and-white coat, we headed down the loft stairs to plug in the coffeepot. Just then, we were hit with another blast from the back soffit.

"What is her problem?" I stammered as we made our way to the front door. Forgoing the coffee, Abe and I quietly snuck out the door and around the east side of the cabin, only to be met with a flurry of black and white feathers headed for the woods as our redhead bobbed to a nearby oak.

I threw my arms up in the air and yelled, "Why must you rivet holes in my cabin?"

The reply was several chirps as bark began flying from the oak trunk to show us her disdain. As Abe and I made our way to the back side of the cabin, we looked up to the ten-foot, flat roof over the utility room to see something crawling, no, several things crawling in and out of a neatly crafted, large, round woodpecker hole.

"Carpenter ants," I said. "That's what she's after... carpenter ants. Looks like we have a job to do after breakfast, Abe."

As soon as we walked back into the cabin, Abe ran to the utility door. After a few snorts and a sneeze, he started growling.

"What is it, Abe? Are the ants inside also?" I reached for the wood latch on the door, and Abe started shaking. I noticed that the hair was standing up on his back, neck, and tail. This wasn't the kind of response I expected for a few carpenter ants.

I began to slowly open the door as Abe rushed past me, driving the door wide open. I heard a very loud crash and a tremendous commotion from the pitch-black room. I quickly flipped the light switch to see a ball of fur come flying at my face. Instinctively, my head flinched to the right, only to catch the doorframe with a loud and painful "thud." Head throbbing, I was met by something that had very sharp claws and was in a hurry to run over my face. The creature landed on my left shoulder as Abraham plowed into my chest, knocking me back across the threshold of the door. My right foot caught on the doorframe, and I lost my grip on the door. Dog, man, and creature from hell ended up in a pile of terror on the floor.

In my pain and surprise, I was stunned to see a very frightened gray squirrel desperately trying to remove itself from the cabin. Both dog and squirrel jumped from window to window. The fur was flying, and so was everything else in the cabin. The lamp by the east window, the bottles of liquor on the bar, and the kitchen utensils on the countertop where all uprooted. To make matters worse, the wife was attempting to pour a cup of coffee while both squirrel and dog came right over the top of the island under the loft and literally took the coffee cup full of coffee right out of her hand.

"Open the door, open the door!" I yelled as they blasted a cloud of ash from the fireplace on their second lap around the cabin.

I hollered for Abe to retreat, but by now he was gaining ground on the squirrel. After what seemed like forever, Dona managed to get the front door open and sheepishly stood holding the screen door. She screamed when both creatures flew out the door at her bare feet. In a flash, the event was over save the heart attack I thought I was experiencing. Wow, more excitement than I wanted on a Monday morning.

After some detective work, I discovered that the flat roof of the utility room had been leaking for quite a while. The board that held up the soffit had begun to rot. The moisture and the soft wood had attracted an ant colony which had taken up residence under the roof. Our annoying redhead was simply feeding off the ants. As she engineered a large opening for access to carpenter ants, a mommy squirrel surveyed that it was just her size. Not only that, but upon further investigation, we discovered that she had moved her family of little ones into the ceiling of our utility room.

After a quick trip to the home store in Muscoda for some treated lumber, we were able to replace the damaged wood on the soffit. In doing so, we evicted our furry residents from the utility room and eliminated the redhead breakfast buffet. Mommy Squirrel was content to rescue her young ones from a nearby tree stump.

Looking back, I guess I'm thankful for the advice from our cabin neighbor Klaus to keep those essential power tools at the cabin. I'm also thankful for the sexy redhead and her engineering skills that led to a leaky roof full of carpenter ants.

*A man travels the world over in search of what he needs*
*and returns home to find it. – George A. Moore*

# There's No Place Like Home

Well, our mini-vacation had come to an end. It was time for us to head home. Buttoning up the cabin, as we prepared to return to the homestead, was bittersweet. It usually took a good three hours to get everything in order. The boats, canoes, and kayaks had to be rinsed out and stored along with the life jackets and sandbar equipment. The garage was locked, the floors were swept, the water was shut off, and the cabin journal was filled out.

Filling out the journal was a time to reflect. It was a mandatory agenda item for each visitor to our cabin. It's like writing a short story of your cabin experience. What you ate, where you went, what you did. It's a chance to reflect back and chuckle at some of the unique things that kept us coming back to the cabin. There was only one problem with filling out the journal – it emphasized that you were headed home! It caused you to realize that you were leaving the wildlife, the river, the sounds of nature, and the stillness that relaxed the mind. I wondered if other visitors to our cabin felt the same way as I did? To me, life seemed to slow down here.

It might just be an illusion, but the days seemed longer at the cabin. There was time to enjoy a sunrise and a sunset with everything in between. There was time for three meals in a day. There was time for hiking and biking. There was time to check the trail cam for wildlife. There was time to explore, time to visit, and time to reflect. There was time to read a book or maybe even write a book. There was time to gaze at the stars and time to sit in the hot tub. There was time to talk to a neighbor walking by with their dog. There was time for life.

What there was not time for was radio, TV, computers, cell phones, and shopping. There was very little time for fixing and yard work, for phone calls and web browsing. Of course, there wasn't time to make money either. Maybe that was why we worked so hard at home…so we didn't have to at the cabin. There was a feeling of regret and wonder in the air, regretting that we had to leave and wondering when we would be back.

Abe seemed to notice when it was time to leave the cabin. He could see all the bags being stacked by the cabin door. His archnemesis, the dreaded vacuum cleaner, was dragged across the floor. The windows were closed and the lights were shut off. Soon he would be found lying in the grass, guarding the car door so as to make sure we didn't accidentally leave him behind.

As we climbed into the car, I had the creepy feeling that we were being watched from the top of the oak trees. Abe quickly lay down on his blanket in the back seat with his head propped up to look out the open window. I could see his nose working. I imagined that it told him a lot more than I could sense. I liked to think that all of his friends were up in those trees saying goodbye. And just like that, we backed out of the driveway and left the cabin and a red sunset in the rearview mirror. All three of us were in a melodramatic haze, and the mood hung in the air like a foggy mist over a sandbar on the river. Just as we pulled away, I heard a barred owl call one last time, "Who cooks for you, who cooks for y'all."

As we drove down the winding road along the river, my thoughts turned to all the things we had left back on the farm. Abe probably wouldn't admit it, but Ada was now his best friend. I'm sure she would have a thousand words to share with him the minute we got home. He would probably just sit and listen. I bet he won't say one word in return.

I knew it had only been a few days, but I was anxious to check on the younger kids we left behind with the teenagers. They would be excited to see Mom and Dad. I bet we won't even get halfway home before the cell phone starts ringing, asking what time we would be home and if we were bringing supper.

Another fantastic reason to go home was the grandkids who would want to visit Oma and Opa to see if we had brought them a souvenir. Even though Abe didn't like his ears and tail pulled, he gets excited when the grandkids come for a visit. I guess it was worth putting up with the rug rats as long as he got to clean the floor under the highchair during mealtime.

While we loved to relax at the cabin, I guess both Abe and I agreed that there's no place like home!

*Life is like a hand-crafted wood flute. It may start as*
*a simple tree branch, but if you work at it carefully and diligently,*
*you can make beautiful music. – Opa*

# Rainy Day Workshop

"It's raining again, Abe," I said as I stared out of the living room window while softly blowing the steam off my hot cup of coffee. As I gingerly took my first sip, Abe jumped up on the windowsill with his front paws to take a look. I guess a more accurate description of the rain was a gentle, wet, spitting drizzle. The slow dark cloud movement of this late August morning hinted that the rain was coming from the east which, according to Grandpa, meant an all-day rain. He would say it was a terrible day for farming but a good day for napping or fishing.

"I don't think we are gonna mow the lawn like we had planned," I mumbled out loud.

"Nope!" Abe replied as he returned to all fours on the carpeted floor.

This morning, Abe's trip out the back door for the call of nature was very short-lived. He didn't circle the vehicles or the arborvitae to see if Jerry had visited during the night or trot up to the barn to check on Ada. No, this morning, he just finished his business and quickly returned to the back porch, scratching at the door. As I opened the door, he shook off the wet drizzle that hung onto the short, black hairs of his back. The threshold got a nice shower as did my bare feet.

"Thanks for that," I stammered, to which Abe shuffled over to his blanket and quickly curled up into a ball of shivering, wet, black dog. "I'm guessing you plan to sleep all day?" There was no response.

After a couple more cups of coffee, I donned my favorite dirty Brewers ball cap with the curved bill and a gray windbreaker jacket from the coat closet and headed to the back door. Opening the door, I paused for a moment, looking back into the kitchen, and called, "Abe, you wanna go outside?" I did not expect a response.

To my surprise, a sleepy, damp dog slowly made his way into the kitchen. He paused for a moment at his food bowl and then continued over and walked out onto the porch, never making eye contact. "Let's spend the day in the barn," I said. "I'll bring your blankie so you can sleep away the rain." As I returned from the living room with his blanket in my arms, I noticed a tail wag of thanks.

The soaking drizzle made everything in nature look somewhat depressed. The green leaves and limbs of the maples were hanging low, burdened with the added weight. The wind was not blowing; in fact, I didn't notice any breeze at all. It was dead quiet outside, eerily quiet. The world seemed paused, at a standstill, and very much at peace. The only sound was the footsteps of man and dog as they made their soggy way to the hayloft of the old dairy barn. No birds were flying, no insects were buzzing, no woodchucks were jabbering.

As I slid open the heavy hayloft door, Abe quickly made

his way over to the woodshop door and shook off the drizzle from his coat. I closed the loft door at first but then opened it back up to leave a twelve-inch opening for dog to come and go as he pleased.

As I walked into the woodshop, I quickly realized that it was unnecessarily cluttered. Odds and ends of many past projects were scattered about the room. Abe waited patiently for me to clear a spot in the corner of the room and meticulously position his blanket. I fluffed his bed into a perfect circle for him. However, he immediately scratched and pawed at the blanket as he turned circles, repositioning everything I had just created.

"Not good enough for you?" I asked. He stopped for a moment to look up at me, wagged his tail, and after several more spins, he collapsed with a groan.

With my hands on my hips, I did my own spinning in circles to look at all the clutter that surrounded me. I decided that I needed to do a bit of repositioning myself.

About an hour later, I had the woodshop back in shape. The hand tools were returned to their holders, the power tools were returned to their shelves, the floor was swept, and the wood scraps were carried out. Nothing like working in a clean and organized woodshop. Hmmm…now what to occupy the rest of my day with?

I noticed one stray two-by-four about twenty-four inches long under the edge of my work bench that I had missed. As I bent down to pick it up, I felt a twinge of creativity come over me. "I wonder if this piece of pine would make a good flute, Abe?" As I glanced over to the corner of the workshop, I noticed that Abe was sound asleep. I was talking to myself now. Oh well. "Let's give it a go," I finished.

One of the many hobbies that cluttered my life was making Native American-style, five-hole, pentatonic flutes. My father had helped me get started in this hobby several years ago by turning out a few cedar flute bodies with his wood lathe. The lathe made a perfectly round flute body. All I had to do was create a wind hole, voice hole, and tune out the finger holes. Today, however, I was excited to transform this piece of scrap two-by-four into a musical instrument by day's end.

The first part of the process in making a Native American-style wood flute was to decide what diameter the interior of the flute should be. Since I was going to use my router to create the inside of the flute, I quickly settled on my 3/4-inch router bit. Next step was to split the two-by-four into two equal halves. Since a standard two-by-four is actually one and a half by three and a half inches in diameter, each half ended up being about one and a half inches square and twenty-four inches long after being split down the center with the table saw. The router was used to dig a half-inch wind groove and a 3/4-inch voice groove in each half. After a little sanding, the two halves were glued together and placed in the wood vice to set. Within an hour, I had a square body ready to be shaped into a flute. Problem was, we had to wait for the glue to dry. As I was tightening the wood vice one last turn, I heard Ada's voice from the doorway.

"You guys are making a lot of noise on a peaceful rainy day. What's up?"

Looking her direction, I said, "Making another flute. I thought you would be hibernating all day with all this warm rain?"

"Lady has to eat," she fired back. "By the way, isn't it

about lunchtime? By any chance, can you and that wet dog get me a sandwich?"

"I guess I need to let this glue harden. What kind do you want this time?"

"Thinking peanut butter and honey if it's not too much work!"

"That actually sounds pretty good myself. Abe, you want a sandwich too?"

At that, I heard a yawn come from the corner of the room as Abe stood up and stretched. Ada immediately walked over and commandeered the warm spot of his blanket and said, "I'll just wait right here. Any chance you could get me a couple apple slices and a piece of that cheddar?"

"I'll see what I can do, boss. Let's go, Abe."

I wanted to finish the flute today but knew that I couldn't work the flute until the wood joint was completely established, so Abe and I took our sweet time making lunch. As requested by Ms. Woodchuck, we made peanut butter sandwiches topped off with some of our own beehive wildflower honey. I cut up a Cortland apple that we had gotten from Oakwood Fruit Farm, sliced several pieces of Carr Valley Wisconsin smoked cheddar, and added a piece of Amish cashew crunch for dessert. After I filled a ceramic soup cup full of Dona's hot homemade vegetable soup that was simmering on the stove, we headed back to the barn. We found Ada exactly where we had left her.

"About time," she said as we walked in the shop door.

I laid a sandwich half on Abe's blanket for the señorita with my left hand, and Abe took the other half of the sandwich from my right. I just smiled when Abe had his consumed in three seconds and stood drooling while he watched Ada take small, dainty, slow bites from her sandwich. Sometimes I think she ate as slowly as possible just to torment my poor dog, but in reality, she was simply savoring each and every mouthful. I sat down on the shop stool and sipped at the hot soup. About halfway through Ada's sandwich, I gave them both a few apple slices. Abe was more interested in the remnants of Ada's sandwich than the apples, but he cheered up when I tossed him a slice of the smoked cheddar.

Abe convinced me that he should share the remains of my peanut butter and honey sandwich by constantly nudging my leg with his wet nose and adding a sharp bark every couple of seconds. Tossing him the last bite, I stood up and said, "Ok, you vultures, I need to get back at this flute. Did that satisfy your taste buds, Miss Ada?"

"That'll do," Ada said as she raised her chubby body off the blanket, brushed against Abe, and waddled out the shop door. "I need a nap."

"How about something new before you go?" I said as I bent down with a bite-size piece of cashew crunch in my open palm. "This is one of Abe's favorites!"

Ada came back into the shop and stood up on her hind feet to take the candy from my hand as Abe let out another bark. "Yes, I've got some for you too, you pathetic canine, just don't swallow it whole like you did your sandwich."

I handed a large piece of our dessert to Abe, hanging onto it with my fingertips so that he had to bite off small pieces at a time. I ate my share with the other hand.

"Not bad," Ada quipped. "Catch you guys later." She walked out the door a second time.

By the time lunch was over and dishes were put aside, the flute glue was well set. I quickly rounded off the square edges of the flute on the belt sander and shaped the mouthpiece. Cutting the wind and voice holes, making a bird, and drilling the pentatonic holes took a while longer since most of this work was done with hand-carving tools. After a good three hours and a lot of filing and tweaking, it was satisfying to hear the first notes emerge from the flute. The haunting yet romantic sound of this pine flute had a plaintive and meditative quality. It was a mystical experience as my own breath brought this dead piece of wood to life, connecting it back to Mother Earth and Father Sky.

The scrap pine two-by-four that I had discovered under my work bench ended up being a very nice rainy-day project flute. By the time it was pitched, it was a little over twenty inches long and tuned to a low F. I finished off the flute by lightly burning the wood with a hand torch. After a dunk in mineral oil, the body of the flute was polished until dry. A thin leather strap was added to keep the bird in place, and Abe brought me two gorgeous feathers for decoration that were donated by a blue jay at the bird feeder. I was afraid to ask him if they were offered or taken.

Just as I finished threading the blue jay feathers to the leather straps, I heard the Mrs. call us for supper from the back porch. With my new flute under one arm and a dog blanket under the other, I slid the hayloft door shut. The rain had stopped, and a few mosquitoes buzzed by my head. The birds were singing again, and there was a warm, gentle breeze blowing. With dog by my side, I proudly strutted into the house to show off my rainy-day project. Greeted by my wife at the door, I haughtily held out my five-hole flute for inspection. She pointed out the door and with five words said, "Boots and wet blanket out!"

*You can't stay in your corner of the forest waiting for others to come to you. You have to go to them sometimes.*
*– Winnie the Pooh*

# Welcome Back

Fall was upon us today, sooner than I expected. September 22nd. While the season of fall in Wisconsin has always been my favorite of the four seasons, as I get older, it seems to sneak up on me faster each year and seems to be shorter than I remember as a kid. Now in my mid-fifties, while I still call it my favorite season of the year, I grumble a bit each year when I know that I do not have things ready for the fast-approaching winter.

There were a lot of great things that I loved about the fantastic fall season. The bugs flew a little slower, and the mosquitoes stopped dead in their tracks. The smells of nature were different in the fall as foliage began to die away, and the cool air seemed to be cleaner and crisper.

At the top of the list was the breathtaking beauty of nature itself. Sure, some years were a bit more colorful than others, but there was something about how the forest green leaves turned to red and orange and yellow and brown that fascinated me. The leaves on the walnut and ash trees would be the first to turn bright yellow, the sugar maples would follow with their vibrant oranges, reds, and golds, and lastly, the oaks would change to a deep rusty red. Even the farm stands were a bit more colorful with carrot orange pumpkins, brown and green squash, and crimson red apples for sale.

Maybe the most intriguing part of fall was how the animals around our farmstead reacted to the shorter days and cooler weather. Penelope was already collecting green acorns for her home above the road when she was not burying them in the front yard. Svetlana was packing away sunflower seeds in the rotted ponderosa, and Bartholomew had moved into the base of a majestic 200-year-old oak tree near the sugar shack. Jerry stopped by most nights to first clean the cat food dish on the back steps and then finish off the sunflowers that Svety missed.

The change of seasons was very apparent in the birds. Many were beginning to migrate, and the air was filled with the sound of Canadian geese and sandhill cranes flying south. The hummingbird feeders were kept full so as to refuel any tiny birds stopping by our place on their way south. The eastern bluebirds had already gone, and most of the robins, along with the goldfinches, Baltimore orioles, swallows, and grosbeaks.

While we tended to lose a lot of songbirds during the fall, we also picked up a little more activity from the regulars. Spike, our resident cardinal, would still come to the feeder every morning at sunrise. The chickadee family seemed to be three times larger, so I imagined that a few northern cousins had arrived down from Canada. The house finches had lost most of their deep red colors and now almost resembled sparrows in the dim light of the morning. Dark-eyed juncos and mourning doves littered the ground under the feeders almost constantly. Rubin still popped up from under the feeder with his beautiful, red, feathered head, and the downy and hairy woodpeckers had become a bit more aggressive as they fought for the most energy-generating feed. I was surprised this morning as I sipped my coffee to also see a couple starlings at the feeder.

Starlings didn't usually come to the feeder by the living room window. In the spring and summertime, they spent most of their time looking for juicy bugs to eat. For sure we saw a lot of them throughout the entire year. They liked to sit on the power lines for hours after sunrise to warm their speckled, black bodies in large flocks called murmurations. I'm not sure who murmured first, but on cue, they would fly down to the front lawn as a group for their breakfast. They lined up wing to wing and marched in a perfect line across the yard, catching anything that moved, such as spiders, grubs, moths, and flies.

Since they liked to stay together in social family communities, we tried to help them out by leaving dead trees standing in the yard and woods around our farm. As long as a dying tree didn't pose any threat to a nearby building, we usually let it die and fall naturally. This conservation technique generated a lot of questions from visitors.

"Why don't you cut that ugly dead tree down and use it for firewood?" one friend asked me a while back. Instead of giving her a lengthy explanation, I simply invited her to stay for supper that night so she could see for herself.

After we had finished a late dinner that summer night, we retired to the back porch to watch the brilliant orange and red sunset while sipping on brandy old-fashioneds. As we sat in our comfortable rocking chairs, I recommended that our guest keep her eye on the dead box elder tree next to the house. It was hopping with starlings. They were popping in and out of empty rotted holes in the tree almost continually. Within a few minutes, she noticed a chipmunk circling the base with a cheek full of birdseed and another one chasing close behind. A pair of nuthatches continually worked the tree trunk, and she pointed out three different woodpecker species pealing back dead bark looking for bugs.

At dusk, as the tree began to be covered in shadows, a mother raccoon emerged from somewhere up near the top of the tree and quietly slipped out of sight just beyond the barn. She turned to me with a smile across her face and said, "Now I understand!"

I explained that the show wasn't over yet and asked her to listen very intently. She moved her chair closer to the porch window and listened with full attention. All of a sudden, her eyes opened wide and she whispered, "What is that? I've never heard that sound in my life!" I explained to her that I had the same question just a few weeks before. A sound so eerie and strange and mysterious but at the same time soothing and tranquil. "Do you have a fairy singing a harmonious love song from deep within that rotten tree?" she joked.

Retrieving the muddled black cherry from the bottom of my glass, I recommended that we abandon our empty glasses of brandy and quietly slip out of the porch. It was dark outside now, but a brilliant half-moon had slid across the sky to illuminate the star-filled night. As we slowly circled the tree, I tapped on her shoulder with one hand and with the other I pointed up to a small five-inch-diameter hole about fifteen feet off the ground. Sitting in the small opening was a brownish-gray owl. Almost on cue, he continued his pastoral call.

"It's a screech owl," I whispered. "We named him Ringtone. He's been here most of the summer. He got that name because the kids think that his singing sounds like a cell phone ringtone."

"That is so cool!" she gasped as she placed her hand on her heart. "Don't ever cut this tree down."

I just smiled as we made our way back to the porch and finished our nightcap. I explained that we didn't burn our brush piles for the same reason. We simply stack them up out of our way so that the critters can use them for homes and so that owls and hawks have something to eat in the winter. Seeing a great horned owl perched in a tree behind the barn in the dead of winter is mighty cool indeed. But back to today…

As I stood in front of the bird feeder this morning, I must have had a goofy grin on my face while I recalled that summer event in my mind. I was probably standing at the living room window for more than a few minutes without taking a sip of coffee. Abe must have thought I was losing my marbles and finally came over and joined me at the window. He had been ringing the back-door sleigh bells for a while, and I had completely ignored that he wanted to go outside. He didn't say anything but brought me back to reality when he brushed my leg and jumped up to the windowsill with his front paws.

"I'm sorry, Abe. I was surprised to see starlings at the feeder this morning."

Abe took one look out the window and began to wiggle

his butt. Soon his tail was going nuts, whipping me in the leg again and again. He jumped down from the window and began to twirl in circles. He ran to the back door and almost knocked the sleigh bells right off the door handle. By the time I caught up with him in the kitchen, he was leaping up in the air with all four feet off the ground. I was confused. Something had him excited, but I couldn't figure it out. I opened the kitchen door, and he did the same, jumping at the porch door. I slipped on the mud boots and set my cold cup of coffee on a windowsill. As I did, I noticed Ada on the top step just outside the door. Now I knew something weird was going on if she came all the way up to the house and even climbed the concrete steps when no food existed. Afraid that Abe was going to plow the innocent woodchuck over in his excitement, I opened the porch window to talk to her.

"What on earth is going on this morning? Abe is about to lay an egg in here."

"She's back, she's back," Ada said excitedly. "Hurry up before she leaves!"

I still wasn't catching on. "Abe, you better calm down. Ada is just outside the door. Sit for a minute while I open the door. Ada, who is back? What are you trying to tell me?"

Ada was squeaking in such a high pitch that I couldn't understand her anymore. She was sensationally excited about something. After a few more seconds, she calmed down enough to get out one word that I could understand, "Stella!"

Almost immediately, something clicked in my brain as I opened the porch door. The starlings at the bird feeder! Abe flew out the porch door, ignoring my instructions. He cleared Ada and all the steps with a six-foot leap. When his nimble feet hit the ground, he never slowed down. His ears were folded back, and he was in a dead run. Dirt was flying, and he was around the corner of the house and out of sight in a second.

"Come on, come on," the whistle-pig squeaked.

She took off after Abraham, and I followed behind her, struggling to keep up. Even I was getting excited now. As I cornered the front of the house, I saw Abe jumping up and down under the bird feeder. There was one lone starling perched on top of the bird feeder, and sure enough, it was Stella. I couldn't believe it. Abe had recognized her through the living room window, and I was embarrassed to admit that I had viewed her as any other front-yard starling.

"Oh my word!" I said out loud. "I can't believe it. Boy, are you a sight for sore eyes!"

Stella flew down and lit on Abe's head for a second and then back up to the top of the feeder. I held out my arm with a finger extended, and she immediately flew over to my hand.

"Welcome home, young lady," I said with a great big grin on my face.

She took off and flew a circle above us and then landed in a nearby mulberry tree next to another bird. She then flew back to the bird feeder, back to the tree, and back to the feeder. Within a few minutes, the second starling flew with her over to the feeder. It was a very young, immature starling. Sure enough, it was her daughter.

For the next hour or so, I attempted to make friends with the youngster while Momma flew from the feeder to my head, to Abe's head, to the feeder. Ada was excited to watch the circus at first, but soon lost interest and tackled a dried-up sunflower stalk under the bird feeder, hoping to find a morning snack.

Never in my wildest dreams did I think we would ever see Stella again, much less meet one of her offspring. I was struggling to get Stella's baby girl to trust me. It was pretty clear that Stella wanted her to fly to my hand. The little girl wanted to go where Momma went, but she refused to land on my hand or my head or go anywhere near that scary-looking dog. After an hour passed, I decided to change tactics.

"Let's give them a few minutes to themselves, Abe. Let's go scramble some eggs."

I didn't want to leave Stella, fearing that she might never return, but something told me she would stay. I had to call Abe several times before he finally followed me around the corner of the house. When I reached the kitchen, I filled his bowl with kibble, but he went immediately to the living room window. I turned my attention to the stove and had a couple scrambled eggs whipped up in minutes. I filled a spoon with grape jelly, grabbed the pan of eggs, and headed for the barn, calling to Abe as I walked out the door. By now, I had an idea of what we might do to help Stella and her little girl.

I knew we still had Stella's wire cage in the barn. Abe found it before I got inside the barn and started to drag it from its hiding place. I dusted it off and straightened the twigs inside. I wiped the mirror off as best I could against the thigh of my jeans. I stole the cat's dish by the barn door and filled it with the eggs, leaving the empty frying pan on the cement floor. I placed a dish of water and the eggs inside the cage. We then carried the cage to the box elder tree by the house. I tied the cage to the lowest limb with binder twine and wired the door open so it could not accidentally close. Finally, I wedged the teaspoon full of grape jelly in between the wire bars next to the open door.

"Let's give them some space," I said as I led Abe over to the porch steps. "You stay here, I'll be right back."

I returned a minute later with a hot cup of coffee. Both of us kept our eyes glued on the box elder tree. Within five minutes, Stella and her youngster were enjoying the jelly by the open door, but it took a good half hour for Stella to brave the inside of her old homestead. After she discovered that she could come and go on her own, she flew in and out of the cage hundreds of times. Another half hour passed before her baby braved the inside of the wire cage, got a first taste of scrambled eggs, and met the pretty young bird in the mirror.

"Looks like we are going to have to add scrambled eggs to our morning routine again, Abe," I said as I patted him on the head.

Ada suggested that we name the young lady Stacey. She instantly became the joy of the farm, well, at least to man, dog, and woodchuck. After a few days of placing eggs in the wire cage, we were able to simply open the porch door. Stacey took her eggs from a small plastic bowl held in my hand while I sat in the rocking chair sipping my morning coffee. Mom would sit on Abe's head and wait patiently until Stacey had her fill of eggs, and then she would finish off the rest. Soon after breakfast was over, they would fly out together and do what birds do.

It sure felt good to have Stella back in our lives. "Welcome back, Stella. Welcome back!"

*Sleeping bags in the woods are to bears*
*like soft corn tacos are to men. – Opa*

# Deer Camp

Today Abe found himself stuck in the back seat of the car again, frustrated at the lack of space he was allowed and surrounded by boxes and boxes of stuff. Every few minutes, I glanced over my right shoulder from the driver's seat and gave him a reassuring smile. I don't think he was very amused.

We were headed back to the cabin. Abe knew that he would be stuck in that cramped space for two long hours. Usually, he slept away most of the trip, but for some reason, he was wide awake today. Maybe it was the sound of tires driving over snow-covered roads that had him concerned. Yesterday was the first snow of the season, and we were blessed with four fluffy inches.

Many people in Wisconsin look forward to the first snow of the season. The first snow means snowmobiles, cross-country skiing, sledding, ice fishing, and snowmen and snow angels. Mother Nature paints a beautiful landscape. Her snow today was hanging on tree limbs like tinsel on a Christmas tree and gently coated the ground with breathtaking white beauty. This mid-November snow blanketed the earth like a warm, fuzzy blanket covering a bed.

I guess I liked the snow and the cold of Wisconsin because it was another radical change in the seasons of the year. Most everyone hoped for snow at Christmastime because it added to the delightful ambiance. However, snow could sometimes catch you off guard. While it gracefully added a cover of beauty across the farm, it also covered all the things in the yard I hadn't gotten around to. Sometimes, due to my own procrastination, there were leaves that hadn't been raked, storm windows that hadn't been put on the house, and dog bombs around the farm that hadn't been cleaned up.

The most annoying thing that the first snow reminded me of today was that every driver in Wisconsin had forgotten how to drive on icy roads. It was like we all needed to be retrained on how to start, steer, and stop our vehicles on the road today. Oh yes, I included myself in this category. I considered myself a pretty safe, reserved, defensive driver, but the first significant snow seemed to bring out the worst of my skills. This may be why Abe could not find restful sleep in the back seat today. The noisy sound of slushy snow in the wheel wells and the anti-lock brakes that had jolted the car a few times seemed to be keeping him alert. He would much rather be up in the front passenger seat so he could better control the situation. He had noticed all of the instruction and correction that was coming from the wife, at the driver's expense, and he was looking distressed. My consoling smiles were not working.

I have to admit that I was a little stressed myself today. Not from my own driving, heavens no, but from all the idiots around me. While I don't wish harm on anyone, I found myself hoping that the last teenager that just about wrecked us as he roared around us like a wildfire would be found in the ditch up ahead. I don't wish injury to him or damage to his vehicle, but he might learn a thing or two if he slid off into a soft, snowy ditch. Paying a wrecker to dig him out of a snowbank might be a great lesson learned. Maybe, just maybe, the old guy with the nervous black dog in the back seat knew a little more about patience and why it was important to go slow on a snowy road. Maybe next time he would cautiously follow behind instead of racing around like we were competing at Road America.

Headed to the cabin we were! The next nine days would be filled with tradition. There would be food, food, and more food. There would be card games to play, beverages to drink, and stories to be told. Yes, you guessed it, we were going to "deer camp."

Deer camp in Wisconsin is a season in itself. Many people, and not only Wisconsin residents, plan all year for these nine days of the gun deer hunting season. It starts on a Saturday and concludes the Sunday of the following weekend. You haven't lived in Wisconsin fully until you have experienced deer camp sometime in your life. It doesn't matter if you are a meat lover or a vegan, an advocate for gun regulation or you carry a concealed weapon, an animal activist or a conservationist, deer camp is for everyone.

Deer camps could be very unique, and I doubted that there were any two that were exactly alike. Each individual deer camp has its own set of rules. At some deer camps, usually a hundred miles away from any civilization, once you arrived, you were never allowed to leave until the nine days were over, not even for more food or beverages or to attend a Thanksgiving Day celebration with relatives. These were the die-hard outdoorsman that took hunting very seriously.

Other deer camps might go out to eat at a bar or restaurant every single day. They leave camp to purchase any sort of modern convenience that they are lacking, such as warm boots or more beer. Some deer camps have a secret ritual or initiation for the new hunter. Others take in any willing participant that graces their camp threshold. Some have a special, designated camp cook, and others take turns cooking meals. For some, it is all about the big, trophy whitetail deer, and for others, it is simply about having a good time.

For us, it was about the latter. "Fun, Food, and Fellowship" would be a good motto at our deer camp. In my younger years, I took hunting a lot more seriously than I do now. Today I would rather shoot a deer with a telephoto lens and hang it on the wall with a homemade red oak frame around it. I still saw the need in conservation so that disease could be controlled in whitetail deer, and I enjoyed a good venison steak fried in butter, onions, and mushrooms, but my desire to hunt for a trophy whitetail to hang on the wall was long over. As we pulled into the cabin yard, I was excited for a full nine days of deer camp. Even Nervous Abe was finally wagging his tail. It was gonna be a great week!

My wife and I had many titles at deer camp, such as Mom and Dad and Oma and Opa, aka Grandma and Grandpa. Since we owned the semi-rustic cabin where we hosted deer camp for our kids, we were the setup and cleanup crew that arrived first and left last. We were the fix-it crew and the food crew, the babysitting crew and the bandage crew. At times, we were even the entertainment crew and the deer processing crew. Having just arrived, we were currently wearing the hat of setup crew.

The setup part might not be the easiest, but it was certainly the most fun. The energy level and excitement level were at their peaks right now. Within an hour of our arrival, the heat was on, the water was on, the lights were on, and the driveway was shoveled and salted. We were eager and ready for our deer camp family to arrive. It would be a crowded cabin this year. There would only be five hunters in deer camp, but we expected a total of twelve bodies and possibly a few visitors mixed in to grace our presence. Our cabin slept six comfortably, so twelve would be a challenge. I sure hoped they all tolerated snoring, cause Abe was a professional.

This was one of those lucky deer camps that had a designated camp cook. She was not only a great cook but a great organizer who didn't take any guff from the boys. Her motto was "help or get the hell out of my way." She had a few traditional meals that we expected each season, and she would usually surprise us with something unique and special. Steak and potatoes were a staple for this meat-a-saurous deer camp, but she would try to sneak in a few salads and veggies along the way. She was *Oma*!

Oma seemed to have the longest list of rules in deer camp, and I guess that was for good reason. There was nothing that a hunter wanted more than a hot, filling, delicious, stick-to-your-bones meal when he got out of his deer blind after three of the coldest, most boring hours of his or her life each morning and evening. Good organization and lots of rules kept this system running very efficiently. There were rules for staying out of the way, rules for stirring the soup, rules for saying grace, rules for passing the food, rules for doing dishes. Get the picture? But dear sweet Lord, look out if you broke one of Oma's camp cook rules.

Cast iron was not only used for cooking in this deer camp. If someone crossed the camp cook, you would instantly see everyone scatter away from the violator. You could be sure that a skillet was coming his direction attached to a very irritated woman. Although it may sound like a complicated thing, once we all knew and followed Oma's rules, this deer camp ran like a well-oiled machine. And there was no greater rule than this: boys did the dishes. Period! Oma cooked, but Oma did not do dishes and neither did any other wife or girlfriend that came along to deer camp. According to Oma, "Girls work hard enough at home, so they do not do dishes at deer camp no matter what. If the boys want to eat, the boys do the dishes!"

Ok, now that we knew a few rules, it was time to have some fun. By the time our first hunters arrived at deer camp, Oma had warm homemade oatmeal cookies, steaming coffee, and sweet chocolate cocoa on the table. The smells inside the cabin were glorious. When you walked in the door, bags were stored, handshakes were followed by hugs, sleeping locations were arranged, and beverages were iced. By the time it was dark, the hunting maps had been surveyed, the hunting gear had been checked and double-checked, and the bellies were full of Oma's homemade soup and baked bread. The cards then came out for sheepshead, cribbage, and euchre. The popcorn was popped, and the beverages flowed. When the camp cook headed for bed, we knew that it was only a few short hours before we heard the coffee percolating and smelled the bacon frying that would wake us all up.

As I mentioned earlier, sleeping arrangements in our small cabin could be challenging with twelve bodies and a black dog. Tonight, a two-year-old had stolen Abe's blanket and had fallen asleep inside his dog kennel, and an eight-month-old infant was asleep in a laundry basket. Six married adults got a mattress and four teenagers would be sleeping on camp cots. I say "sleeping," but I doubted that the teenagers would sleep. They were pretty excited about tomorrow's hunt. If they were anything like I was in my youth, they would lie with their eyes closed but their mind wide open, unable to sleep. Sleep would come to them tomorrow after lunch during the Badger football game.

Abe was ecstatic! He has had the best eats of his life in the last three hours at the cabin. Everyone found their own way to sneak him a snack or two, scrub his ears, and scratch that hard-to-reach spot in the middle of his back that he loved so much. If he was really lucky, that was sometimes followed by a belly rub and a piece of buttery popcorn after a hand "shake." He wasn't too sure about having his blanket commandeered by a snotty toddler, but finding out that the Mrs. would let him sleep on the bed tonight was a pleasant compromise. No doubt he would be the first one snoring.

Unfortunately, morning came too soon. The hunters, three guys and two ladies, wolfed down coffee that was too hot to drink, a few strips of candied bacon that were too hot to eat, and biscuits with sausage gravy as they scrambled to get out the door. They looked like they were getting ready for war. There were knives and bullets and camo face paint and flashlights and so many layers of clothing that some were unable to bend over and lace their own boots. I guess they hadn't given any thought as to how they were going to climb a tree with all that long underwear, sweatshirts, coats, mittens, and hats under that blaze orange exterior. It was opening morning, and they were anxious and excited to get into the woods well before daylight.

Within a half hour from the time the deer slayer wannabes headed out the cabin door, we began to hear gunshots along the river corridor. Abe was glued to my side at the sound of the first percussion. The cold, 25-degree, clear morning should keep the deer moving, however, there was no buck-fever for Abe and me this morning. We had been assigned to the breakfast dishes and were sternly reminded not to soak the cast iron bacon skillet.

While I intended to split some wood for tonight's fireplace, we began to hear that a crisis had developed and were quickly chosen to rectify the situation. The ladies had discovered that a few shopping items were missed. Most of the time, the ladies were more than willing to head to town for supplies, but the twenty-mile drive on a frozen, snowy road had enlisted the help of the boys this morning. I argued that maybe we should wait until later in the day to let the road salt melt more snow off the roads, but I guess it was an emergency this morning. It seemed that we accidentally forgot to bring extra rolls of toilet paper. I quickly found the car keys, and the last thing I heard as we headed out the door was, "Get a box of chocolates too."

We called our cedar wood cabin "rustic" because it did not offer the accommodations of a modern house. However, I was thankful it did have the basics in running water and an inside flush toilet. I appreciated our rustic cabin even more on the way to town. Sure, we saw expensive pickup trucks parked in front of very expensive third-wheel campers, but we also saw deer camps that sported primitive canvas tents and outhouses.

"I bet the ladies in those deer camps aren't making the men go after chocolates this morning, Abe," I quipped as we drove by a super fancy, class-A recreational vehicle. Abe kept silent, still concerned about gunshots, and we soon pulled up to the five-n-dime on Main Street in Muscoda.

I guess I wasn't surprised to find a man dressed in blaze-orange sitting at the soda counter. He had a young hunter with him not older than twelve or thirteen. It was less than two hours after opening deer hunting hours, and the young lady was already frozen solid. The only place for them to warm up was the local department store. I felt a tug in my heart for both the kid and her dad and a feeling of relief knowing that I was past that part of my life. All of my hunting kids this year were old enough to go into the woods on their own and had the luxury of coming back to a warm, well-stocked deer camp when they were cold. I asked for a large box of assorted chocolates from under the counter and grabbed the jumbo economy pack of quilted toilet paper. I smiled at the dad and gave him a "been there, done that" thumbs-up before rejoining Abe back in our vehicle.

"I think we have the best deer camp in Wisconsin this year, Abraham!" Abe instantly high-fived my glove with his left paw and wagged his tail in agreement.

*Like the seasons of the year, life changes frequently*
*and drastically. You enjoy it or endure it as it comes and goes,*
*as it ebbs and flows. – Burgess Meredith*

# My Egg

As we wrapped things up at deer camp this year, I am happy to announce that the witty whitetail once again outsmarted the homo sapiens. In so doing, there have been some new stories created, and they will be used to rub salt in the wounds of the mighty hunter again and again, year after year. That is one thing that is fair game at deer camp, all the should-have, could-have stories from the previous years. The deer will get smarter and the antlers will get bigger every time the story is told. Just like the fish that got away gets bigger with each conversation. I guess that is part of our human nature, to brag a little, to point the blame on someone or something else, and to pick on the frailty of one another while having a good laugh at their expense.

As we pulled into the driveway of the farm, I laughed out loud and pointed to the garden. Standing dead center in the middle of a row of frozen brussels sprout stalks was a ten-point buck having a late afternoon snack. If only the mighty hunter had stayed home and hunted in his own backyard. If only. Oh well, that's just the way that nature has its own laugh once in a while. He stood there in the garden with a proud, arrogant demeaner. You could bet that he knew that he was safe for another year. With a few flashes of his beautiful white tail, he mocked us and elegantly bounded over Ada's log and disappeared into the woods.

Speaking of Ada, I was surprised that she had not poked her head around the barn while we unpacked the car. It now being late November, she might just be hibernating. We might only get to see her on warm, sunny days for a few months. I bet the farm will be a lot quieter without her jabber. Most of nature seems to be falling asleep in the cold these days. Even my own outdoor activity will change in the days of December as we round the corner into January. I wonder if other people compartmentalize the times and seasons of the year like I do.

In my mind, the year is like a big oval. It is not perfectly round, rather the year in my brain is almost egg-shaped and viewed as an egg rests on a table. Right now, as we head into December and get ready for the Christmas season, we are rounding the far-right corner of the oval. The top, flat side of the oval is January through May, and the left curve of the oval is June through July. The bottom, flat side of the egg is August and September. Curving up on the right side is October to December. I guess this may seem a strange way to think about the months of the year in Wisconsin, but this thought has been with me since my childhood. I don't know where the thought came from, but I do know why it is oval-shaped.

In my own confused mind, the flat sides of the oval are the long seasons of the year. The months of the year that seem to drag on a bit longer than others. The left and right side of the oval are much shorter in length and represent the seasons in my life that go by quickly. I suppose this is a weird way to think about a calendar, and I'm not sure that I can explain it with any certainty or intelligence. All I know is when someone mentions a time of the year, I can instantly picture where that lies in the egg of my life.

Earlier, I explained that the season of fall is my favorite time of year. Here in Wisconsin, I consider fall to go from September to late November, but it goes by so quickly that it is merely the bottom right corner of my egg. Again, in late spring at the end of May up through June when I am itching to get outside for canoeing or camping before the mosquitoes take over the world, time rounds the upper left corner of my egg. Both of these seasons go by so quickly that I often long for them to return. I know I spend way too much time planning for these corners of my life because I am often frustrated that little is accomplished when they sneak up on me.

As a contrast to the short favorite seasons of my year, the flat, elongated top and bottom of my egg are the seasons that take forever to end. The long, cold winter months of January, February, and sometimes March sit on top, and the hot, long days of July and August with their bugs and humid temps sit on the bottom of my egg. Don't get me wrong, I find things to enjoy in those months also, but to me they take forever to end. In the spring, I can't wait for the days to get longer and temperatures to get warmer, and in the last days of August, I can't wait for the first frost to knock out the bug population. Weird, believe me, I know. I don't think I have ever heard another person explain a year exactly like my depraved mind has compartmentalized the months of the year. But as I said, we were just about to round the top right corner of my egg.

*Our minds, as well as our bodies, have need of the out-of-doors.*
*Our spirits, too, need simple things, elemental things, the sun and the wind*
*and the rain, moonlight and starlight, sunrise and mist and mossy forest*
*trails, the perfumes of dawn and the smell of fresh-turned earth and the*
*ancient music of wind among the trees. – Edwin Way Teale*

# Sunshine and Moonshine

I was suddenly awakened by the swing of the bedroom door. It opened and closed without a sound as if someone or something had entered the room. The lack of light in the room did not help to solve the mystery. "Oooffff," I gasped when two large, black-and-white paws took the air from my chest. "Good morning, Abe...is it that time already? Is it too much to ask for five more minutes? Did you plug the coffee in?"

As my feet hit the floor of this old farmhouse, I cringed at the feeling of a very frigid hardwood floor. I reached back under the covers, contemplating the return into the warm cocoon from which I had just emerged. However, as Abraham stuck his head back inside the bedroom door to see if I was following, I reluctantly stumbled forward to begin our day. I say "our" day and not my day, because well, if you have read any part of this book you know what I mean.

Bells ringing, coffeepot plugged in, kibble, scrambled eggs, Spike and Rubin, the usual. By now, you know the routine. The only thing missing recently was Ada and Sunflower, Svetlana and Penelope. They were all enjoying a long winter's nap in semi-hibernation. Abe and I saw them only on unusually warm, sunny days and only for a few minutes. It was pretty quiet on the farm right now.

Abe and I were headed out to the sugar shack for a secret project today. We had been saving up and looking forward to this day for a long time. This was going to be a special day. As I said, a secret day. Today was the one day of the year that dog and man would spend behind closed doors. We won't let anyone else in, we won't answer the cell phone, and the only time we will leave is for a sandwich and a potty break. I'm guessing that every person on this earth has a few secrets in their life. Things that are not shared, save maybe only with a very close friend or a spouse. This one was ours.

"I better grab the flashlight, Abe," I said as I opened the porch door against a still dark sky. "We don't want to give away our secret by turning on the lights."

Soon, we were quietly rolling open the large wooden door on the side of the barn. I clicked on the flashlight and scanned the large, empty haymow. I wondered what this timber frame once looked like full of loose hay. The iron, horse-drawn hayfork still stood perched up in the highest peak of the barn. As the dim light of my flashlight glanced across it, there appeared eerie, elongated shadows on the faded barn-board wall that looked like something from a horror movie. As I moved the light around the room, a cold breeze caught the back of my neck and sent a chill down my spine. The shadows inside the barn seemed to be moving all by themselves. I paused for a moment to listen to the dead silence of the empty barn.

Abe didn't seem to be affected by the same silly, haunting feeling I was experiencing and quietly walked into the darkness without reservation. It startled me as he brushed my leg, and I let out some kind of inhuman sound that startled the both of us. It's funny how the fear of dark, spooky places has that on the human soul.

Abe stood there and stared at me for a few seconds, confused at my state of mind, but soon walked out of sight into the dark barn by himself. I could hear the clicking of his nails as he walked up the stairs by the woodshop. By the time I reached the stairs, I could hear that he was scratching at the canvas tarp we had hidden behind the maple syrup buckets. I shined the light in his direction, which only illumined his reflecting, green eyes. Another chill hit me.

I took a few final sips of coffee and set the ceramic cup on a barn beam. After moving a few maple pails out of the way, Abe helped me remove the tarp to reveal our secret stash of equipment. To the average person, this pile of precious metal would probably look like the remnants of a plumbing disaster, but to us, it was a work of art. A quick survey of parts and pieces and we were ready to start moving.

"Looks like it's all here, old boy," I said. "Let's get this over to the sugar shack before the sun gets up."

Within fifteen minutes, we had everything inside the shack with the door closed securely behind us. I hung the flashlight from a rope that suspended from the ceiling, and it swayed back and forth, creating spooky shadows on the wall but giving us just enough light to assemble our moonshine still.

Yep, you heard me right, and now you know our secret. We were about to put together our homemade moonshine still. You must swear an oath of silence before we go any further! We can trust you? Ok. Within the hour, we would have everything put together. Don't tell now!

The concept of a still is actually a very simple device consisting of a heat source, a copper cooking pot, a few coils of copper tubing, several thermometers, and a condenser. The wood-fired rocket stove heats the copper pot above it, the tubing at the top of the pot collects the vapor, and the condenser turns the steam back into a liquid which is collected at the end of the four-foot exhaust tube. Oh sure, there is a little more to it, like using hydrometers and thermometers, but the process is fairly basic. Heat the mash just below boiling, collect the steam, and turn it back into liquid. That, my friend, is how you make moonshine.

Unfortunately, craft distilling is frowned upon in most of the country and particularly in Wisconsin. There are mainly two reasons for this: taxes and safety. First of all, making your own whiskey, vodka, or brandy is heavily regulated and taxed by our government. They want to be sure that they get their own fair share off the finished product. And secondly, safety is the other reason why craft distillers need a license. Pure moonshine is very combustible, and we were using an open wood flame as a heat source. That is a very good reason to be careful.

You might be thinking that Abe and I were doing this illegally, right? Au contraire, my dear friend. I said secret, not illegal. There exists a loophole that allows us country folk to explore the craft of distilling grains or fruit into alcohol. By applying for a Fuel Alcohol Permit, Abe and I had become a legal craft distillery. The alcohol we hoped to produce today would be used for fuel, not for human consumption. "Then why all the secrecy," you ask?

I guess this really isn't a secret thing that we do, rather something we try to do under the radar as to not draw attention. It's kind of my own private thing. Something that I just don't want to share with the public. By now, you have probably realized that I like to be different than the average Joe. Most of my hobbies are unique. I keep honeybees, make maple syrup, craft wooden flutes, play the ukulele, and distill fuel alcohol. Does that make me unique or weird? Maybe I'm both. Distilling, for me, is done in secret like in the days of prohibition just because I want to do it that way. That's it, just because. If a friend finds out that I own a still, they instantly think it is illegal. I do not admit it or deny it, I just let them draw their own conclusion, and I ask them to keep it a secret.

"Abe, the sun is coming up. We better get the wine and mash out of the basement before we get caught," I said as I winked at my partner in crime.

Five days ago, we had boiled some crushed corn and barley malt and added some brewer's yeast. This was our mash that would be converted to alcohol. After several days of fermenting, it makes a product called low wines. This is strained and put into the copper still pot. Abe and I slowly bring it up to temperature, keeping it just below boiling. The covered copper pot directs the alcohol vapor into a copper coil that is submerged in snow and ice water. The cool temperature then condenses the vapor into a concentrated alcohol and is collected at the end of the copper tubing. Voilà, we have moonshine!

In addition to the corn mash today, we were excited to try our hand at making brandy alcohol from the Concord grapes that the Mrs. fermented this fall. One carboy had a bitter taste that she didn't like, so we planned to distill it into brandy fuel, save the charred oak barrels.

Well, as the morning breaks, the sunshine is finally out along a clear, blue sky, and there is not a cloud in sight today. The nostril hair freezes with each breath of the cold five-degree-below air. As I leaned against the door of the moonshine shack, I reflected back on the year. It would be just one long month before we dug out the maple syrup equipment and started this whole year all over again. My thoughts turned to all of the animals on the farm tucked away in their winter dens, sound asleep.

While deep in thought, standing motionless in the doorway, good ol' Abe came over to join me. Climbing up on the woodpile next to me, we ended up side by side, elbow to elbow, staring out across the farm. For a moment, we both just enjoyed the cold, still air standing together as partners, best friends, and life-long companions. His black nose worked the frozen air, telling him things I could only imagine. Did he think like me, wondering about our friends Sunflower and Ada? For a second, I thought about striking up a conversation with him, but instead I was content to simply enjoy looking out across the farmstead in silence. Smiling to myself, as I recalled the fantastic adventures we had enjoyed together, I knew that he would say very little anyway. I imagine that we both think alike, wondering what kind of adventure this new year would bring and what new and exciting friends we would meet.

The constant, rapid drip off the copper condenser tube, which had been steady for the last two hours, was beginning to slow. The hydrometer said we collected about 80 proof alcohol. Spending time with Abraham on our secret project today produced both sunshine and moonshine at the same time. As I turned from the door to remove the copper still from the rocket-stove, I brushed against his side. He watched me for a moment, then climbed down from the woodpile. Catching me off guard, he jumped up and rested his black-and-white paws against my chest. With one simple word, he summed up our friendship.

"Wooof!"

# Opa's Epilogue

Well, it's about time I wrap this narrative up. It's been a beautiful year of adventure and new discoveries! Who knew that animals could talk? Well...I guess I'd challenge you to ask any dog, cat, or horse owner that very question. You betcha they can talk! And I bet if you listen, listen really close, and be patient, real patient, you might be able to hear, not just the domestic kind, but the wild creatures attempting to communicate with you. Maybe you won't be able to use human words like I can with Abe and Ada, but I bet you will be able to understand each other in many other ways. Listen to the movements and the little noises. Make eye contact. Move slowly. Be gentle, be observant, and be available.

This story is just a little way of sharing with you some of my everyday life. Every tale is absolutely a true tale as I remember it. Each event came from a real-life event. Each adventure was a real-life adventure. The names are real, the people are real, and the animals are real. The opinions are, well, my opinions. Take them or leave them. All that I ask is that you pay attention! Maybe you will watch the birds on the bird feeder a little closer now. Maybe you will notice the taste of the syrup on your pancakes and find out where it came from. Maybe you will step out of your comfort zone to find that new adventure once in a while. Maybe you will think twice about crushing that house centipede, because his name might be Pete and he just might very well be trying to deliver a message to you.

So here is our farewell.

I wanted to ask Abraham if he had any last words, but I can see his legs twitching while he sleeps by the woodstove. He must be chasing raccoons out of the woodshop or the squirrels off the roof while he dreams. Maybe I'll just let him rest for now. Ada, on the other hand, would like you to know that she is now the proud mommy of two cute young'uns tucked deep in her den. Abe and I see her on warm days in the vegetable garden, eating the frozen brussels sprouts or digging up frozen carrots. She would also like you to know that it's ok to leave your salad scraps by the barn door, that peanut butter and honey sandwiches are "to die for," that people falling on ice is hilarious, that woodchucks are man's best friend, not dogs, because they are smarter and smell better, and well...about a billion other things.

Farewell, my friends. Enjoy this spectacular creation God has given us. Always listen to things around you, try to learn new things once in a while, and live life to its fullest!

*The END*

# Acknowledgements

I would like to recognize the staff of this awesome publishing company for believing in my work and rescuing this novel from the depths of my computer. It was Lauren Lisak, my editor, that afforded her patience, encouragement, and professionalism, bringing what was typed into something readable.

In addition, I give appreciation for my brilliant wife, who is not only a fantastic spellchecker but a resourceful thesaurus. Thank you, my love, for believing in my work and for wanting me to succeed as an author.

A quick word of gratitude is due for my dear friends that offered their cottage on Lake Wisconsin where I put pen to paper. Coffee at sunrise and wine at sunset exposed me to your generosity and benevolence.

Finally, I would like you to join me in thanking the pets in our lives. For it is the love and companionship of my own dog Abraham that inspired this book. Therefore, I ask in my best northern accent, "Holy cry-yin, ya der hey, give dem a big ol' Sconsin bear-hug what-nat for me, by golly!"

Hopefully you'll take the time to find the title of this book on the World Wide Web or Facebook or Instagram and post a picture of you and your pet holding a copy of it. I would love to meet the pets that communicate with you in your own daily routine.

## About the Author

Mark Snyder, better known as Opa, grew up in Sauk County, Wisconsin. After college, he enlisted in the United States Air Force, where he met a beautiful young lady that lived across the hall from him in the barracks. Together, they supported the 69th Dragon Tactical Air Command (TAC) squadron at Moody Air Force Base near Valdosta, Georgia, supplying munitions for F-16 Falcon Jets. They have been married over thirty years and are blessed with six children and a quiver full of grandchildren. They own and operate a business in Wisconsin and are well known for their specialized work with computerized organs, pipe organs, and digital pianos. In their spare time, they operate a hobby farm in Jefferson County, Wisconsin, where they enjoy a plethora of wildlife. They have several pets that occupy their time and communicate with them on a daily basis.

CPSIA information can be obtained
at www.ICGtesting.com
Printed in the USA
LVHW091035191119
637663LV00051B/2740/P

9 781645 380924